LOST & FOUND

LOST & FOUND

A Treasure Trove of Folk Tales

ELIZABETH GARNER

Illustrations by Phoebe Connolly

unbound

First published in 2022

Unbound
Level 1, Devonshire House, One Mayfair Place, London W1J 8AJ
www.unbound.com
All rights reserved

Text design by PDQ Digital Media Solutions Ltd.

A CIP record for this book is available from the British Library

ISBN 978-1-80018-123-6 (hardback)
ISBN 978-1-80018-124-3 (ebook)

Printed in Great Britain by CPI Group (UK)

1 3 5 7 9 8 6 4 2

For my parents
Who set me out on the long roads with their blessing.

&

For Pascale
Who came along for company.

With special thanks to Linda Davis, a patron of this book.

Three apples fell from Heaven

One for the listeners

One for the storyteller

And one for those who told the tales before us

CONTENTS

Foreword by Hugh Lupton   xi

The King of the Birds   1
The Riddles of the Crossroads   9
The Twisted Oak   17
The Wits of the Whetstone   29
Little Stupid   49
Little Dog Turpie   61
The Roots of Fortune   71
Johnnie-He-Not   85
The Black Bull's Bride   95
Stealing the Moon   121
The Troll King's Sister   131
Ashypelt   143
Just Jimmy   157
Little Sparrow   167
The Coal Companion   185

Notes on the Tales   193
Bibliography   219
Acknowledgements   223
A Note on the Author and Illustrator   225
Supporters   227

FOREWORD

Joseph Campbell, in his commentary on *Grimm's Fairy Tales*, has written: '*If ever there was an art on which the whole community of mankind has worked – seasoned with the philosophy of the codger on the wharf and singing with the music of the spheres – it is this of the timeless tale. The folk tale is the primer of the picture-language of the soul.*'*

Here is a new book of old stories. Elizabeth Garner has drawn from the great European and Russian wonder-tale collections, and the folk tales of the British Isles, and made an intertwined gathering of folk narratives. Like all of us who work with this material she's allowed herself to be a medium, a conduit for the lost voices of all those who have carried the stories before her. It's no small responsibility.

Traditional stories have long histories. They've been fashioned over countless generations, each teller leaving a trace of himself or herself – a turn of phrase, an aside, an episode – embedded in the tale. For most of their long lives they have been told, held in the memory and turned on the tongue. They have been precipitated in oral cultures where the written word – if known at all – has been the province of the few. The countless tellers who shaped and carried the tales have largely been forgotten. They've slipped into the hallowed ranks of 'anon'.

* Joseph Campbell – from 'Folkloristic Commentary', *Grimm's Fairy Tales*, Routledge and Kegan Paul, 1985.

What we're left with are the names of the collectors: the folklorists, academics and poets who have set the stories – just as they were disappearing from common usage – onto the page. We talk of the Brothers Grimm, but we forget the tailor's wife Frau Viehmann who *'told her stories thoughtfully, accurately and with wonderful vividness'*. We talk of Italo Calvino, but we forget the illiterate Sicilian grandmother Agaruzza Messia: *'the more she talked the more you wanted to listen'*. We talk of Katharine Briggs but forget the gypsy Eva Grey who *'sweeps you along without pause from beginning to end, words pouring from her lips in a torrent, her hands, her eyes, her face, her whole body reinforcing their meaning and significance'*. The permanence and respectability of the printed page has trumped the ephemeral moment of the word on the breath.

An oral culture only carries what it needs. With no libraries or digital storehouses, it depends on the capacity of human memory. What can't be held in the head and hand is cast aside. Survival skills and local knowledge are passed from parent to child, from craftsman to apprentice. And miraculously, alongside the practical stuff, the stories and ballads have been too precious to be discarded. The folk tale – that mysterious, funny, frightening metaphorical picture-narrative of magic and transformation – has been remembered. It has come down through the generations. It has been needed.

I'll leave the academics – psychologists, historians, literary critics and folklorists – to argue why this might be so. To anyone who's heard one of the old tales told with skill, from the heart, the answer is simple: it touches us, it moves us. These ancient concentrations of human experience, distilled and matured over hundreds of years, have the power to awaken something essential. What is it – a half-remembered question, a veiled feeling, a loss, a longing, a deeper justice, an animate understanding, a precarious truth? Tolkien has called it a 'consolation'. He cites, in particular, a story that appears in this collection as 'The Black Bull's Bride':

> *when the sudden 'turn' comes we get a piercing*
> *glimpse of joy... that for a moment passes outside*
> *the frame, rends indeed the very web of story, and*
> *lets a gleam come through.*
> *Seven long years I served for thee,*
> *The glassy hill I clamb for thee*
> *The bluidy shirt I wrang for thee,*
> *And wilt thou not wauken and turn to me?*
> *And he heard, and he turned to her.*

Let's look at another of the stories Elizabeth Garner has included in this collection. She calls it 'Little Stupid'. It is one member of a family of tales and songs that appear and re-appear from Northern Europe to India. In the Aarne Thomson Folktale Index it's listed as no. 780, 'The Singing Bone'. It tells of a murder and the disposal of the corpse, it tells of a musical instrument that is made from the body parts (or a plant that grows from the grave mound) – sometimes it's a flute, sometimes a fiddle, a harp or a set of bagpipes – and it tells of the terrible denouement when the voice of the victim sings its truth through the instrument's music. The victim is usually the third son or the little sister, killed by jealous siblings. The image of a flute singing with a dead girl's voice is arcane, it resonates with our inner storehouse of mythic dream-images (what Jung called the Collective Unconscious). But at

---

* J R R Tolkien, from 'On Fairy Tales', *Tree and Leaf*, Allen & Unwin, 1974.

the same time it chimes with a very contemporary fascination with forensic investigation. The DNA test that solves an old murder sets old bones singing. The faces of the older sisters or brothers when the truth is sung are the faces of those guards from Belsen or Auschwitz, suddenly exposed after holding their dark secrets for decades.

An oral story only speaks to 'now', to the moment of telling. Its setting may be the secondary world of 'once upon a time', but its core concerns have always had to be contemporary. If it had been whimsy or nostalgia it would have been forgotten. The fact of its survival attests to its always having been, in some way, relevant. However much the external conditions of the world rearrange themselves, the human heart remains a constant. And this is what the folk tales address – love, death, betrayal, constancy, trickery, luck, jealousy, courage, transformation.

All the tales in this collection have spent the greater part of their lives in the memories and on the tongues of storytellers. Elizabeth Garner grew up in a household that is steeped in story. The first time I met her (in the 1980s) was on a visit to her parents' house in Cheshire. She must have been about eleven. She had a transparent apple and a silver saucer. She showed me how to spin the apple on the saucer. That was then. Now she's a novelist, editor and teacher. In this book she has returned (like John Chapman in 'The Roots of Fortune') to the warp and weft of the old tales. In the tradition of Hans Andersen, James Stephens, Angela Carter and Neil Gaiman she's taken the spindle and shuttle from the dead hands of the old forgotten tellers and woven – with the written word – a fresh cloth from their stories. Like all of us who work with this material she's negotiating that fine line between the ancestors who stand behind and the eyes and ears of those who are meeting these gnarled and sappy stories for the very first time. It's the job of each generation to make the old tales speak afresh, and in this collection she's fashioned a vibrant web. Prepare to encounter beast-husbands, troll-wives, stout hearts, cannibalistic witches, the birds of the air, cruel sisters, shape-shifters, sun and moon, all the denizens of the Secret Commonwealth, the Devil, Death himself and (outwitting them all) the redoubtable Jack. The stories are illustrated and counter-pointed by Phoebe Connolly's exquisite wood engravings.

So take courage, traveller, the boat is trim and seaworthy, the new-sewn sail is taking the ancient wind, the tide is on the turn... but be careful, with a crew like this anything could happen. Bon voyage.

Hugh Lupton

THE KING OF THE BIRDS

One morning all the birds of water, land and air came together in a forest clearing to decide which amongst them should be crowned The King of the Birds. Great Eagle stepped forward, wrapping his golden cloak of feathers around his chest.

'Before we elect our sovereign leader,' he said, 'we must first consider what makes a bird a bird.'

'I know! I know!' squawked Proud Peacock, nodding his head as if his crown of bright blue plumage was proof that his station was already decided. 'It is the fineness of our feathers.'

His small grey wife hid her head beneath her wing as he fanned out his tail of a thousand eyes and shrieked.

No sooner had Peacock said his piece than Prattling Parrot flew up to the lowest branch of a nearby oak tree, his emerald-green feathercoat outshining the new Spring leaves.

'Vanity!' he cried, in a voice stolen from the Bishop of the Lands. 'Vanity of Vanities! The true measure of a worthy soul is the humility of character allied with an agility of the mind.'

The harsh, honking laughter of Gobbling Goose rang through the air as Peacock folded his tail behind him and slunk into the shadows.

Parrot gave a bow and puffed out his fine-feathered chest. 'Surely, my flock, you deserve a King who can match the quickness of his wits to the wonder of his wings.'

No sooner had Parrot said his piece than Bold Kingfisher swept down to the river, flitting and flickering, with his sky-blue back, his belly the colour of sunset and the grey glinting needle of his long beak plunging down into the water. He came up carrying a silver slip of a minnow and flew back to the clearing, placing the flailing fish on the ground before the crowd.

'My dear companions,' he said, 'am I not already half-King within our company? Whereas poor Parrot has a title which holds no more value than an echo. He has won mankind's favour with his mimicry and his coloured coat, but what has he gained? To be kept as a pretty pet, forever grateful for the meagre morsels cast upon the floor of his crafted cage?'

On the branch above, Parrot shuffled back into the canopy as if he could conceal his shame within the embrace of the leaves.

'Surely,' said Kingfisher, flicking his beak with a swordsman's flourish, 'what makes a bird a bird is the skill of the hunt.'

No sooner had Kingfisher said his piece than the air above trembled, and there, landing in the clearing in swift and soundless flight, was Wise Owl, folding his broad brown wings to his back. He turned his head this way and that, staring the chattering crowd into silence. There was a trembling mouse trapped beneath the curved crescent of his claw.

'There is the hunter who dazzles with his flame-feathers,' said Owl, 'and there is he who uses the skills of stealth and swift execution. Tell me, is it the showman or the able assassin who makes the strongest leader?'

Owl took the mouse up in the sickle hook of his beak and swallowed it down in one gulp.

Kingfisher retreated to the riverbank, as quick as a flash of light. Chaffinch, Pipit and Goldcrest scuttled to the back of the crowd and hid behind the wide wings of Swan.

No sooner had the tip of the mouse's tail slipped down Owl's gullet than Cunning Crow strutted forward and cocked his head.

'No better champion of the forest floor, my friend,' he said. 'But the true hunter is he who ventures far beyond the limits of his own lands to seek his fortune.'

Crow flew up to the wind-whipped top of the oak where he had his nest. From there he tipped out treasures. A blue ribbon, a silver coin and a golden ring all came raining down upon Owl's head. Crow cackled from his perch.

'He who steals from mankind is surely the quickest and cleverest of all the birds and should be crowned accordingly.'

No sooner had Owl shaken aside his humiliation and soared up into the sky and away, than Savage Sparrowhawk came plummeting down the wind like an arrow, his tailfeathers folded like fletching, and he grabbed Crow's nest from the treetop in passing. As he landed in the clearing, he crushed that bowl of twig and moss to dust beneath his talons. Chaffinch, Pipit and Goldcrest crept further inside Swan's embrace. As Crow dragged his shattered home away, Sparrowhawk fixed the crowd with his yellow eye.

'A True King is he who has a voice made for battle,' he said, 'who can call his clan to him over land and sea to fight at his side.'

He opened his beak and gave out a piercing cry that echoed across the forest and back again.

No sooner had Sparrowhawk spoken than Nightingale flew high above his head and began to sing. It was a song of joy and longing, laughter and tears, and it was as if the whole forest held its breath to hear it. But only for a moment. Before Nightingale could state his case, the other songbirds flocked to join him – if it was the sweetness of the tune that would gain the crown then they were not going to concede Kingship uncontested.

Warbler, Songthrush, Blackbird and Woodlark jostled Nightingale aside, all pushing against one another for the most superior perch. The air was full of calls and whistles but as one competed with another there was no beauty to it, only conflicting cacophony.

Then Great Eagle opened his beak and called out, 'Enough!'

The force of his cry threw the songbirds from their branch; they dusted themselves down and flitted away from the clearing as Great Eagle stepped forward once more.

'My dear kinsfolk,' he said, nodding his head this way and that, as if he were bestowing a blessing, 'are you truly so ignorant of your own natures? I who have travelled far and wide across the lands can tell you true, none of the qualities over which you quibble and quarrel are what makes a bird a bird.

'In the Kingdom of all that creeps and crawls, the insects of the forests and the scale-skinned creatures of crevice and crag, there is more pure shining colour etched upon their bodies than can ever be found upon our feathers.

'In the wide-sweeping deserts and the cruel lonely mountains there are beasts of the land more practised in cunning and wilder at the hunt than we could ever claim to be.

4

'And in the depths of the tumbling oceans, there live the Grey Ancient Ones, who have more beauty and sorrow in their songs than anything we could ever sing out to the sky.

'There is only one thing, my friends, that makes a bird a bird and we carry it upon our backs.'

With that, he drew himself up to his full height and shook out his wings. The span of them dwarfed the trunk of the oak and they shone as brightly as the sun.

'So let it be decreed,' said Great Eagle, 'that he who can fly the highest shall be crowned The King of the Birds and let there be no further argument about it.'

The air was alive with the sound of wings upon the wind as all the birds of the world rose up in a great flock.

Laughing Lark flew straight and true, the morning dew on her breast falling away as she circled the boundaries of the clouds and sang.

'Here I be! None better than me!'

But she soon spun herself dizzy and fell back down to earth.

Ragged Rook flew far, far, and further than far, until the forest below shrunk to a small speck of green that he could swipe aside with his claw. Beyond it stretched the reaches of the world – the deserts, the oceans, the rocky ranges of the mountains, the many Kingdoms and their castles.

He cried out in mockery of his fellows flying below.

'Caw, caw, caw, I can see it all!'

But as he did so, he boasted all the breath from his body and fell back down to earth.

One by one, all the birds tired and abandoned flight in favour of the sanctuary of solid ground.

All except for Great Eagle, who had of course commanded a contest that favoured his own particular strength. He beat those huge golden wings, slow and steady, and climbed forever upwards, carried by the tides of the air until he reached the tallest of all the mountains. He held his wings as steady as a sail as he circled it three times, calling out.

'I am The King of the Birds! I am! I am!'

Then he felt something stirring in his tailfeathers.

And there, flitting through the sky behind him, came Little Jenny Wren. She had hidden upon Great Eagle's back for the long journey and her strength was unspent. She was quick and spry, and Great Eagle could not catch her as she flew up to the mountain top, the highest point of the known world. There she perched in victory and sang.

'Here I sit! Highest it! Highest it!'

And so it was that Wren was declared The King of the Birds.

Great Eagle could not bear the shame of being tricked by such a small plain bird and he was quick to anger. He drew back a golden wing and struck a savage blow against Little Jenny Wren. She tumbled from her stone-throne perch, went plummeting down the whole height of the sky, tumbling to the forest floor, her wings clipped.

Since that day, Wren has never been able to fly higher than a hawthorn bush, whilst Great Eagle can be seen soaring up to the curved dome of the sky, chasing clouds for his sport.

You will find Great Eagle spreading those golden wings of his far and wide across this world – from the lectern that holds the Bishop's Bible to the coat of arms of Kings, to the sign that swings above the inn to welcome you. But if you ever find yourself lost on a twisting path in the forest, in need of some cleverness and courage and a clear, sweet song to set you on your way, you would do well to seek out Little Jenny Wren.

The Riddles of the Crossroads

J ack was sitting on the back step of his Old Mother's cottage staring out at the far horizon, waiting for his Fate to come over the hill to claim him.

He had dreamed it out in many directions, the way his story might unfold. He could do a favour for a passing tinker and he'd get a purse brimming with silver coins for his trouble. A magic purse, no less, that would never run empty. Or he would save the honour of a wandering Princess. Then she'd fall in love with him and take him back to her father's castle and they'd be wed. Or perhaps a club-footed, iron-toothed troll, all hair and fists, would come hurtling out of the hillside and run rampage through the valley. Jack would defeat the fierce invader and he'd be a Hero of the Land.

The more days that passed without incident or opportunity, the more restless Jack got. So one morning he took his Old Mother's freshly baked loaf from the top of the stove and he went to see the Henwife. They broke bread together and he told her of his plight.

'There's a tale of a man who finds gold in his own backyard,' she said. 'But his name is not Jack.'

Jack thought of how wide the world was, and how little of it he knew.

'I've no fear of adventure,' he said. 'But I'm in sore need of advice and direction.'

'Fate waits for us all at the same spot,' said the Henwife. 'Where North, South, East and West meet.'

Jack kissed his Old Mother farewell and set out on the long roads.

He walked and he walked, sleeping in hedges and ditches, sharing food and fire with the tinkers, the merchants and the men who were down on their luck. They all traded their tales between them, to ease the long journey.

Each time Jack asked for direction to assist him upon his own particular adventure he was given the same reply. The man who sets out on the promise of a Henwife's riddle is as foolish as he is innocent. Jack should go back the way he came and be content with the life he's got. Better that than to waste his years searching for a place that's not to be found on any map of this world.

Still, Jack walked on.

Until one day he came to a crossroads with a signpost set in the centre, cutting up the clouds like a compass. Leaning against it was a tall, thin Gentleman, dressed in a long dark coat. He had a fiddle tucked under his arm and a black hat upon his head that put Jack in mind of the stovepipe in his Old Mother's kitchen.

'Kind Sir,' Jack said, 'may I trouble you with a question?'

'Certainly,' said the Gentleman. 'Is it a great question or a lesser one?'

Jack thought of all the folk that he had met upon his travels and how not one of them had been able to offer him an answer.

'I suppose it must be a great question,' said Jack. 'The rest of my life depends upon it.'

'Then I would be happy to assist you,' said the Gentleman. 'All I ask in return for a true answer is that you pay me back in kind. Nine lesser questions of my own, set against the singular greatness of yours.'

They shook upon the agreement.

The Gentleman had a firm grip. His nails were long and filed to a point.

'Then tell me true,' said Jack, 'where is the place that North, South, East and West meet?'

The Gentleman took the bow of his fiddle and drew a perfect circle in the dirt around where Jack stood.

'Simple, my friend. Where else but beneath your own feet?'

Jack laughed, and then he stopped.

He was stuck fast, frozen inside that circle.

Then he understood the nature of the Fate that he had met, and his blood ran cold.

The Gentleman turned and whispered in Jack's ear.
'Now as you did swear to me,
Answer my questions, three times three.
If you cannot tell true these nine,
Then your very soul be mine.'

Then he tucked his fiddle beneath his chin, struck up a tune and sang.

'What is taller than the tree?
And what is deeper than the sea?
What is sharper than the thorn?
And what is louder than the horn?
What is greener than the grass?
And what is smoother than the glass?
What is longer than the winding way?
And what is colder than earth's clay?
And what is there, seen, told or heard,
More dreadful than the witch's words?'

Jack looked into the Gentleman's eyes. They were as black as pitch.

And there he saw the world unfold accordingly.

There was a forest, set beside a deep blue sea. The floor of that forest was tangled with thornbushes.

There came a King on a noble steed, blowing upon a hunting horn as he vaulted the brambles. Then the King and his huntsmen were returning victorious, dragging a black boar across the verdant lawns of the castle grounds.

A fine feast followed, with toasts raised in crystal goblets.

Into the hall there came a woman. She cursed the King and his company for the slaying of the most beloved of all her companion creatures.

Instantly, all the people of the court became statues of clay that crumbled before the King's eyes. The castle followed, rent to rubble at his feet.

His Kingdom beyond the tumbled walls was now a barren desert. There was nothing but the road ahead, twisting like a serpent across the land.

Jack could feel the ground beneath his feet opening up as the

Gentleman played his fiddle, faster and faster.

Jack shut his eyes and sharpened his wits. He thought of all the tales of the long roads. The tales of this world, and of the hidden places above and below it.

Jack took his thoughts, and he set them to the Gentleman's tune.

'Heaven is taller than the tree
And Hell is deeper than the sea.
The hunger of a jealous mind
Pricks sharper than the thorn so fine.
The shame of the beloved's scorn
Cries louder than the hunter's horn.
The envy that stews deep in the blood
Runs greener than the field or wood.
The flattery that does honest truth surpass
Is smoother than the shining glass.
Colder than the clay of any land
Is the touch of Death's sure hand.
But love is longer, in both the finding and the keeping
Than any winding way of fortune-seeking.
Dreadful though the witch's words may be
The Devil is worse. And you, fine Sir, are none but He.'

The fiddle stilled its tune.

Jack gathered all his courage and looked directly at the Gentleman as he sang out his final verse.

'Your riddles thus solved, the wager is won.
With your true name I command thee – Devil, be gone!'

Two handsome horns came twisting out of the sides of that stovepipe hat. Hands and feet became claws and hooves.

There was a terrible tearing as the long coat was rent asunder by steel-scaled wings sprouting from a buckled back and a tufted tail unravelled beneath.

Savage Satan let out a great roar which shook both land and sky as he departed in a flash of fire.

Jack scuffed away the circle that had held him.

Then and there, he vowed he would not fall foul of the self-made snares of jealousy, shame, flattery or envy. Nor would he risk the trading of his own heart for that of another.

Nor would he set his gaze upon a far horizon and dream away his days until Death laid its hand upon his shoulder.

Instead, Jack pledged that he would set his mind only to whatever unfolded directly before him. Step by sure and steady step, he would be the constant master of his own Fate.

Then he took a penny from his pocket, set it spinning beside the signpost, and the road that it fell upon was the road that he took.

The Twisted Oak

O nce there was a farmer's daughter and her name was Jeanie.

It was Christmas Eve. Midnight Mass was over, and she was standing at the crossroads outside the church. There was the long road to the North, winding down through the village and up the hill to the farm. Then there was the short road to the East – across the stile, through the woods, over the fence and she'd be back in her warm bed in no time. So this was the road that she took.

A full moon hung low in the sky to light Jeanie's way. The pealing of the bells grew quieter as the trees closed in, but Jeanie had no fear of the forest or anything within it. She knew every twist of the tracks, every sound that could play tricks on the mind of a traveller – from the hooting of the watchful owl to the scamper of the quick fox in the undergrowth. But this night, drifting down the wind, there came something else. A long lamenting tune that was both the saddest and the sweetest song she had ever heard. It called to her, and she followed it.

It led her away from the road home and down the darker paths, until she came to a place that was unfamiliar to her. There was a clearing with a tall, twisted oak at the heart of it.

It stretched so high that the stars became the bright blossom of the branches. And there, leaning against its broad bark-buckled trunk, was a man.

He was dressed in a velvet suit. A broad-brimmed hat cast shadow over his face. His hair was as dark as the fallen night. He had a fiddle tucked beneath his chin, the head of which was carved into the shape of a grinning imp, with oak leaves forming his features. The bow had a silver tip that flashed through the darkness. Jeanie could not be certain if the man was playing the music, or the music was playing the man.

Then the tune stilled, and he looked up. His eyes were the colour of new-grown grass.

Jeanie saw that he was not one of the village folk – he was from somewhere else.

'I am in need of assistance from a quick and clever girl,' he said. 'I wonder, is that you?'

'Quick and clever enough,' said Jeanie, 'not to take on a task without knowing the nature of it or setting a price.'

'It is but a simple piece of farm work.'

He pulled a velvet pouch from his pocket and tipped out a cascade of silver coins into Jeanie's palm.

'Half upon agreement, the other half when we are done.'

Gazing down on the fortune winking up at her in the moonlight, all Jeanie could think of was the damp of the milking shed and the stink of the straw as she shovelled it and how much she wished for a life beyond all of that.

They shook hands on the agreement. The man's hand was white and soft, and Jeanie felt ashamed of the roughness of her work-worn skin.

The man struck his bow against the trunk of that twisted oak three times. As he did so the bark split and shifted, and a doorway opened. The man took Jeanie by the arm and led her inside.

Jeanie found herself standing in a vast golden hall. A vaulted ceiling stretched above her head like a second forest. There was a table running the length of the room, piled up with a fine banquet. Seated at it was a party of lords and ladies, drinking from goblets brimming with wine and they were all making merry.

Jeanie's belly ached and her mouth watered, and she reached out her hand, but the man stopped her.

'This is not for you,' he said.

Not one of the carousing crowd looked at Jeanie and the man as they walked past. It was as if she and her companion were ghosts to this company.

At the end of the hall was another door, guarded by two handsome black hounds, tied to their posts with chains of silver. Jeanie reached out her hand to pet them but again the man stopped her.

'This is not for you,' he said.

He led her to a tapestry hanging on the far wall. Embroidered upon it were flowers of the forest, some of which Jeanie knew and some of which she did not. The man pulled it aside to reveal a staircase made of copper and he guided Jeanie down below, step by ringing step.

The stairs led into a candlelit cavern.

In the centre of the room was a tall four-poster bed. On the bed was a woman, full-bellied and with skin as grey as ash.

'This is for you,' said the man.

Jeanie had seen this before, at calving. She knew well enough that once the cold sweats come crawling, if the new life doesn't get out quick it's a bad end for both. She had also heard tell what can happen to a midwife who births death.

She reached out her hand to the woman's belly and this time the man let her.

'It wants turning,' she said.

'And you have the skill,' said the man. It was an order rather than a question.

Jeanie thought of the black hounds above, the feasting crowds and the way that bark-buckled door had shut so swiftly and tightly behind her.

'Not with you at my shoulder,' she said. 'There's women's work and there's men's work and they are not for mixing.'

The man smiled, but there was little kindness in it.

He took a jar from his pocket. It was cast of gold and in the shape of an acorn.

'When the child comes, smooth this ointment into every last inch of its skin. But on no account place any of it upon your own person.'

Jeanie did not think to question the impossible nature of this instruction. All her attention was upon the immediate task before her.

For hour upon hour, Jeanie pummelled at the belly of the weeping woman. But life is life – it has urgency and intention. The baby righted itself and came into the world shrieking and perfect. A bonny boy, with his father's dark hair and his mother's blue eyes.

Jeanie pooled the ointment into her palm. It glistened like the shimmer of a rainbow.

She worked it over every inch of him: between his toes, behind his knees, into the crease of his elbows, inside the perfect shell of his ears. As she did so his howling turned to coos of contentment. When she was done, she gave him to his mother. No words passed between them, but Jeanie saw such sadness in her eyes, she had to look away.

Then the full weight of the long night came upon Jeanie in a great wave. She was ready to sleep where she was standing. She rubbed her right eye, her fingers still slick and sticky. When she opened that eye again the room and everything in it was changed.

The bed before her was nothing but broken boards stacked up with straw, tented in by twisting tree roots.

The boy clawing at his mother's breast had nothing bonny about him.

His skin was dark and wrinkled. He stared at Jeanie. His eyes shone emerald green and his gaze was not that of a newborn.

Jeanie stumbled, caught within the rotten root cage. And there, suddenly beside her, was the man. He was lifting his son up and pressing him to his cheek, against a face that was now sallow-skinned and ancient, like against like.

'Well done, my quick and clever girl,' he said. 'Fair work deserves fair payment.'

What had been a fine velvet pouch was now a scrap of sacking. He placed it in Jeanie's palm, curling his fingers around her own. Dark against dark, like against like, her ointment-slick hands now as gnarled and knotted as blackened bark.

But Jeanie thought of the World Above and all she loved in it – the wide-open meadow that blossomed each Springtime with a wealth and wonder of wildflowers. She did not flinch. Instead, she thanked him kindly and took the arm that he offered to her. His coat was nothing but rags.

Up the stairs of rootstock they went, and through a torn tapestry of dead leaves. Sat sentry at the other side were two giant black rats, straining against their cobweb-collared leashes.

But Jeanie thought of the World Above and all she loved in it – the way her favourite cow let Jeanie rest her forehead on her flank as she milked her. She did not flinch. Instead, she walked steadily past the rats' spitting and snarling.

She found herself in the hollow heart chamber of the oak, the golden roof now broken branches and stinking moss. The table was piled up with grey offal and mouldering bread. The wrinkled and tatter-clad tribes raised glasses of bilge water and drank deeply.

Jeanie felt the bile rising up in her throat.

But she thought of the World Above and all she loved in it – the salt-sizzled bacon in the skillet, the smell of her mother's baking, the fresh water drawn from the well. She did not flinch. Instead, she held her head high as she walked through the rotten banquet, keeping her gaze fixed upon the door ahead.

She felt the hard hammering of her heart as the man tapped on the door three times, and it opened. There was the forest beyond, and freedom.

Jeanie stepped across the threshold, but the man still had her arm, and there he held her, one foot in this world and one in the other.

'Mark my instruction, my quick and clever girl,' he said. 'Utter one word on this matter to any living soul and all your good fortune will crumble into dust.'

Then he loosened his grip upon her, stepped back and the skin of the tree sealed shut.

The Christmas bells were still chiming as Jeanie raced through the woods, leapt the fence and was in through the door of the farmhouse and drawing the bolts tight behind her.

She emptied out her pockets and purse – no silver there, nothing but dry leaves. But it was a plant she knew – the grey, flat, round seedcases of the Honesty flowers that grew far and wide across the forest floor at Springtime.

For other girls, that might have been the end of their story. But not for Jeanie. She was quick and she was clever.

She blinked, and for a moment there was bright silver winking up at her.

She blinked again – nothing but dead Honesty.

She placed her hand over her right eye and there was the pile of coins. To the unseeing and the unknowing, she had indeed been gifted with riches, if she chose to take them.

In the weeks that followed, Jeanie soon learned the trick of keeping her enchanted eye hidden behind the curtain of her hair so all that she saw was the truth of the world she had returned to. The rich red sky of dawn, the soft lowing calls of the cattle, the golden churning of the buttermilk all carried a beauty that she had never noticed before.

But as the year turned and the hard labour of harvesting came round, with it returned the temptation that had caught her in the moonlit clearing. There was a world beyond the fields and the fences and she would be a part of it.

So she took herself to market and bought lace gloves, a dress fit for a lady and the jewels to match. She kept her enchanted eye tight shut as she counted out the coins. No matter how much she took from that purse, it was always full. She became quite the talk and the beauty of the village and before the turn of the next year it was wedding bells that she was walking out of the church to, on the arm of the Innkeeper's son.

As the ale flowed, quick and clever Jeanie traded the bad coins alongside the true and soon she and her handsome husband were rich. The years passed and just as her eye accustomed to only seeing the world she wanted to see, so did her mind. She bore three sons and with each birthing she thought a little less about the captured woman laid out on her bed of straw and the savage suckling of that thing that Jeanie had coaxed into being: part boy, part not. By the time the sons of her own sons came into the world, that chamber of roots and moss was a half-remembered dream, shifting and uncertain.

It was the birth of her first granddaughter that took Jeanie back to the market that day. She was wandering the stalls, but nothing was quite good enough for the baby girl that had been given her own name: Bonnie Jane. Not the bunch of red ribbons, nor the puppet of the wooden hens that pecked and clucked upon the tabletop, nor the blue glass beads that shone in the sunlight.

Then she heard it. A song of both sweetness and sadness, calling across the air. It was a song that she felt she had known all her life, and yet she could not place it.

There, standing in the corner of the market, was a raggedy man, with a tattered wide-brimmed hat pulled over his face and a fiddle tucked beneath his chin. She could not tell if the man was playing the music or the music was playing the man.

She dropped a handful of coins at his feet.

The tune stilled.

Jeanie looked down at the head of the fiddle and an imp of the oak grinned up at her. Then she remembered.

She clamped her hand over her right eye. The market corner was deserted, only empty air before her. But she felt another hand on the lace of her glove, prising her fingers away from her socket one by one. And the last thing she ever saw with that eye was a sharp bow tip of silver coming in close and quick.

The night of the next full moon, Jeanie took her bag of false Honesty and went back out into the woods and followed the darkest tracks until she found herself back in that clearing. There was the twisted oak and its vast branches holding up the sky. She took a trowel from her pocket and dug down, deep into the roots, and buried her treasure. She called out into a night that she hoped was listening.

'True sight for false silver,' she cried. 'And let this be an end to it.'

She waited there until dawn but no one came and nothing changed.

She never ventured into the forest again.

At the inn, there are still tall tales told about the ghost of Blind Old Mother Jean who was robbed at the market by thieves who took her eye along with her fortune. It is said that she wanders the lodging rooms above, weeping blood and tears, troubling the nights of any dishonest man who crosses the threshold of that place.

THE WITS OF THE
WHETSTONE

On the morning of the first of May all the folk of the village had danced and drunk the month in as dawn broke over the high hill. Now they were gathered together at the threshold of The Eagle and Child. On the village green the well was brimming with blossom. The Marigold, Sweet William and Forget-Me-Not charmed the air and brought about a new kind of intoxication.

Under the Innkeeper's instruction, the Blacksmith was hoisted up on the broad shoulders of the Cooper. He loosened the links of the swinging inn sign, then re-holed and re-hung it. The Child kicked skywards, his fat fists holding tight upon the talons of Great Eagle. The noble bird was now rendered as powerless as a folded pheasant set for bracing, the golden wings falling useless from his back. The crowd cheered as one to see it – the order of the world thus turned upside down.

Then the Soldier came striding through the gathered company, rolling out a huge, handsome whetstone as if he were commanding a cannon upon a battlefield.

The Innkeeper's challenge sounded across the air.
    '*He who has the sharpest wit is worthy of the sharpest*

knives. So let the best and boldest liar claim this fine whetstone as his prize!'

The Merchant set up a table by the door of the inn and made note of the men and women who presented themselves. He drew up a list of boasts and the bets to match them.

Jack steered his Old Mother to a seat upon a nearby tree stump as the Innkeeper set out the rules of the contest.

'Good folk,' said the Innkeeper, 'I have spent my live-long life quenching the thirst of the honest man and the scoundrel alike. I've heard truth spun to falsehood for the sake of romance, reputation and remuneration, and plenty more besides. I will declare the Most Absolute Liar of this fine company directly and let none of you contest the title.'

The Mountebanks of the townships were the first to stand, jostling shoulder to shoulder beneath that swinging sign, wheeling out their wonders. There was the peacock's feather declared as the princely plumage of the Firebird, the pumpkin offered up as the mare's egg, the crab claws claimed as the diabolical digits of the Devil.

They were swiftly laughed out of the contest. These touted tricks were tales that had been played out across generations of the village folk. Inherited apprentice-piece illusions, passed from grandparent to child, to illustrate the importance of looking at the world with close and careful attention, in order to find a clear path through it.

Then it was the turn of the women to argue out their

impossibilities. The Baker's wife and the Tailor's sister brewed up a great debate between them about the sweetest and the sourest substances known to man and the worth accorded to each.

Then the stoop-shouldered Henwife stepped forth and stilled the argument. 'I'm not here for pursuit of profit,' she said. 'But I come with fair warning. Goodness in this world is proved a blight in another. And it will go badly for any fool who forgets it.'

Her words put a quietness on the crowd, until a tatter-clad Tinker stepped forward, with his little dog yapping at his heels.

'Good folk,' he said. 'I tell it to you as it happened to me.

The moon had fallen from its sky-fixing and the night was as black as a bag.

I'd taken the longest of the long roads, right into the thick heart of the forest. I could not pass a thread of silk between the trunk of one tree and its neighbour.

'Then I spotted a chap sat in the middle of the path, three miles ahead. He was milk-eyed blind, and he was lacing up his battered boots with sand-spun string.

"Do you have the time about you?" I asked him.

He pulled a watch from his pocket and studied it.

"Midday on the very dot," said he.

I thanked him and I went on.

'I followed that road, until I walked my way into the middle of last week. I came to a gatepost. There leaning against it was a deaf and dumb man playing a snail shell and all about his feet the mice and the worms were partnering up for the Longsword Reel, striking stakes of straw.'

At the front of the crowd, the Shepherd Boy pulled a whistle from his pocket. The village folk kicked up their heels and so did the Tinker as the tune squared and played out.

The Innkeeper applauded.

'Tell on, good Sir,' he said. 'In the same true fashion.'

The Tinker raised his glass and grinned.

'I quenched my thirst with a cup of sawdust, then I asked a question of that merry minstrel.

"How far to the nearest village?"

"Five thousand miles," he said. "And the road is not a kind one."

I thanked him, then took a hop, skip and a jump and I was at the village boundary.

'There was a dark field. In the centre of it stood a naked man, scattering corn the long breadth of it in a single throw. Wherever the seed fell the bonny barley grew up as fast as a flash, and whether he or I were the most grateful for it, I couldn't say.'

Jack's Old Mother cackled into her cups and the Tinker tipped her the wink.

'Then up out of the cornfield came a hare the height of a horse. The naked chap pulled a gun from his pocket and shot it. I skinned the beast with a needle, built a bonfire of green grain stalks and roasted that long-leaping leveret. We shared the feast out between us and gobbled up the lot in one mouthful. Then I went on my way.'

The Tinker opened up his coat and there, pinned to the lining, was a pair of rabbit's paws, strung tight together. The crowd laughed as one, as his little dog leapt up barking and biting as if to rip the feet from their fixings.

The Innkeeper stepped forward, but the Tinker raised his hand.

'There's long tales and short tales,' said the Tinker. 'This one's both and neither. Unless you're calling me out as a liar, Sir?'

'Another man might, but not I,' said the Innkeeper. 'Tell on.'

'I left that field, walked round in a circle and I came to a crossroads I'd not seen before.

Then from the North came a man with no hands, pushing a wheelbarrow stacked full of gold. From the South a chap with no legs came running after him, shouting, "Stop, thief!" I dropped my breeches and let out a great fart that blasted the barrow apart and all that gold came falling out.

We quartered it up and each took an equal share.

The thief filled his pockets, the boss man filled his boots, we shook hands on the deal, and we went on our separate ways.'

Again the Innkeeper stepped forward.

Again the Tinker raised his hand. 'Some tales take a straight road and others do not,' he said. 'This one is both and neither. We've not got to the start, the middle, or the end of it yet. Unless you are calling me out as a liar, Sir?'

'Another man might, but not I,' said the Innkeeper. 'Tell on.'

'Well as you folk all know,' said the Tinker, 'I'm nothing if not a good Christian. Off I went in search of the church, so I could give thanks to The Almighty for the blessing he had chosen to bestow upon me.'

He clasped his hands and lowered his gaze.

At the back of the crowd, the gesture was echoed: a bowed head, fingers folded before a red-robed belly.

'It was the fanciest chapel I'd ever seen,' said the Tinker. 'Built from a matchbox with a thimble for a steeple. There were a thousand folk gathered inside for a wedding. I took a seat beside a poor old fella, who was weeping fit to split his waistcoat. He was a hundred years if he was a day. When I asked him what had got him so heartsore howling, he told me.

"That's my dear old Grandad up there at the altar," he said. "He's a simple chap, never loved a woman in his live-long life, and we rubbed along well enough together just him and I. But now he's had his head turned by that one and she's shut the door against me."

'There's many kinds of disadvantage in this world, but to be set out of hearth and home by a cruel mistress is the worst of them. So I emptied my pockets of that barrow-fallen fortune and wished him good luck and good comfort and went on my way.

'As I was walking out through the graveyard, I came across a dead man carrying his own coffin. He was having a hard time of the task, so I set my shoulder to it alongside him.

We got to his hole and chucked the casket down. Before he followed it, he shook my hand and gave me his final earthly instruction.

He told me true, I was to seek out the place of work of his own dear brother and he'd put me right for my kindness. For there is no man more generous than the Innkeeper of The Eagle and Child.'

The crowd roared with laughter and applauded as one.

The Innkeeper passed a flagon of ale to the Tinker and cast a mutton bone at the feet of his little dog.

'A fair price for a fine story,' said the Innkeeper.

Then the whistling Shepherd Boy stepped forward.

He took a silver shilling from his pocket and began tossing it, palm to palm, as he spoke.

'Good folk,' he said, 'I tell it to you as it happened to me. It was but a month past, I was up the slopes with my flock and my old Elsie. There's nothing that dog likes better than the chasing of a fast-flung stick. I was that caught up in our game that I fair forgot the matter of the herding. Those sheep may as well have grazed their way into the heart of that high hill for all I know because they surely weren't to be found anywhere upon it.

'Elsie was kicked to her kennel, and it was twelve lashes of the rope for me. Then the boss man said I could go straight to Hell and make my bed there for all he cared. So off I went.'

The fat-faced Farmer gave out a bark of laughter and the Shepherd Boy tipped him the wink.

'It wasn't such a bad place. There was a good roaring fire and plenty of cinders to fashion a bed from.'

The crowd shifted with prickled-shouldered unease. Some folk were smiling, but some were not.

The Innkeeper nodded to the Shepherd Boy.

'Tell on, good Sir,' he said. 'In the same true fashion.'

The Shepherd Boy nodded back in kind and kept his coin spinning.

'The only trouble was the blasted imps. I'd had quite enough torment for the day at the hand of my master. So I went directly to the Devil for negotiation, with not so much as a prayerbook in my pocket for protection.'

The Shepherd Boy made a quick sign of the cross before him, catching the shilling at each intersection.

At the back of the crowd, there was the swift square glinting of a golden ring, echoing the gesture.

'One thing I'll say for Old Satan is that when it comes to the striking of a bargain, he's the most honest master I've known.'

The Innkeeper stepped forward, but the Shepherd Boy shook his head.

'The tinder of the tale is set, but the fire's not taken,' he said. 'Unless you are calling me out as a liar, Sir?'

'Another man might, but not I,' said the Innkeeper. 'Tell on.'

The Shepherd Boy grinned and tossed that shilling higher and faster. It flitted through the air like a starling made of silver.

'I was offering my services in return for the use of the Hound of Hell. Now all the tales you've heard about him are true enough. He's a magnificent old beast, black as night, and he's got eyes as red as fire and three rows of saw-sharp teeth. He's the height and heft of a bull and as swift as a rat down a gutter. And he stinks worse than the midden and the cowshed put together.

'But as you know, my friends, any dog follows the nature of his master. So whilst the Devil's got the old boy chained to a post with seven shackles, it's no wonder that he's got a temper on him. The moment I slipped the poor chap's chain he was licking the hand that freed him. Then all it took was the whistle, the come-bye and the gather and he's herded the imps right back in their cage.'

The laughter rippled round the crowd in a whisper.

The Innkeeper stepped forward, but the Shepherd Boy shook his head.

'The flame's caught but the riddle's not yet roasted,' he said. 'Unless you are calling me out as a liar, Sir?'

'Another man might, but not I,' said the Innkeeper. 'Tell on.'

'Now Old Satan was as happy as a pig in muck, because he can set to sharpening his instruments without any of those bad little lads messing with his diabolical workings. And I got my head down by that fire, with the Hound of Hell stretched out beside me, and slept the whole night through.

'Then would you believe it, next morning, the Devil's offering me a permanent position. I tell you, I was sore tempted – a man likes to take work where he's best appreciated. But then I thought of my dear Mother and what it would do for her reputation if word got out, so I declined his kind offer and settled for payment instead.'

He turned his face to the sky now, addressing the coin rather than the company.

'The Devil gave me an honest guinea for an honest piece of work. Trouble is, it's been lying that long in the coffers of Hell, all the gold has been burnt from it and it's too hot for holding.'

At that moment, as quick as thought, he caught the spinning coin in his hand and threw it at the Innkeeper's feet.

'All I'm after, Sir, is that you trade it in for a cold one, from the coffers of The Eagle and Child.'

The Innkeeper crouched down on his haunches. He touched the shining shilling and drew back his hand quick.

Then he pulled a gleaming gold guinea from his pocket.

'A fair price for a fine story,' he said as he handed it over to the laughing lad.

Jack strode forward. He had a rusted scythe stuck in his belt and he struck the tip of it against the whetstone, calling the chattering crowd to silence.

'Good folk,' he said, 'I tell it to you as it happened to me. It was but a year past, my dear Old Mother and myself were plagued by the sudden appearance in our own backyard of a most troublesome and unruly beanstalk.'

The crowd groaned as one and the Innkeeper stepped forward, placing his hand upon Jack's shoulder.

'Come now, Jack,' he said. 'You know as well as the next man there's no place for such worn-out several-spun stories in this contest.'

'That I do,' said Jack with a grin. 'But do not be so hasty, my friend. It goes the same way with the getting of a fortune as it does with the brewing of the beer. There's nothing achieved in this world or any other without preparation. The golden-egg goose and the humming harp and the swift skyfalling of that Big Old Fella came on the third day's climbing. This is the tale of what went before all of that.'

The Innkeeper shrugged his shoulders.

'Then tell on, good Sir,' he said. 'In the same true fashion.'

Jack counted out the passage of time on his hand as he spoke.

'The first day was spent slipping and sliding and all I had to show for my efforts was my red-raw skin-stripped shins. The second day, I fashioned myself a pair of stout iron boots and they gave me anchor and purchase. So off I went, up that buckled beanstalk, and I was halfway to the cloudtops when I came upon a bees' nest as big as a barn. There was no going round or over it; the only way was through. So I knocked on the door and in I went.

There was Mistress Queen Bee sat upon her throne of honeycomb. She came at me quick sharp with her sting set out. I parried my sword and we had quite the fencing match.'

Jack swiped his scythe this way and that and the crowd applauded the pantomime.

'I got round the side of her, and I cut her wing clean off. That nest upended and I was tipped from it, with the wing falling after. That Royal appendage fell heavy upon me and I was stuck fast. Then along came a fleet-footed Flea, and we struck up a bargain. He'd be my swift saviour on the condition that whatever piece of luck I next found myself blessed with, he'd take it as his full and fair payment. So I got up onto his back and off we went.

'Flea took a great leap, and we were across the wide sea in a single stride. We landed in a field of corn. Just like it went for my good friend the Tinker, this was no ordinary field. As his grain grew swift, mine grew gold, each and every ear of it.

It gleamed wide and ripe across that land, all the way to the far horizon.'

At the front of the crowd, Jack saw the Merchant take out his pocketbook and note down the particulars.

'Are you calling me a liar, Sir?' asked Jack.

The Merchant arched an eyebrow but spoke not a word.

'Another man might, but not I,' said the Innkeeper. 'Tell on.'

Jack wielded his scythe once more, aping out the harvest.

'I cut the field clean and was up to my neck in gold. Now as all you good folk know, I'm not a man who breaks a bargain. That treasure was friend Flea's for the taking. But he had neither pockets nor boots for the carrying of it. So I took my sword and sliced him in two, quick and clean, turned that flea-skin inside out and fashioned it into a sack. I filled that fleabag up to the brim, but I hadn't the strength to lift it.

'Then who should come flying through the air but a flock of golden geese, hollering out for their missing brother. I called back in kind, telling them that if it was a lost soul they were after, there was none more abandoned than poor Jack.

Now Gobbling Goose is the kindest and most courteous of all the birds, and it goes double with the Golden ones. They hauled me and my sack of treasure up with them. They made a bed with their backs and those feathers were as soft as they were shining.

'We had a fine wind behind us and across the sea we went as swift as a whistle. There was the valley, the village, and I could see my Old Mother's house below. But I hadn't reckoned on the beanstalk.

My fine-feathered friends had no choice but to break ranks or be caught by it.

The fleabag split, and that wonderous corn rained down riches across the land, like The Almighty Himself was casting down his manna from above.'

At the back of the crowd, there was a flash of gold in the sunlight – a crucifix held up to the Heavens as if to ward off the downpour.

'I went tumbling after,' said Jack. 'But luck was on my side. That good wind caught and carried me out to the high hill. But a man cannot fall from such a great height without consequence. I went hammering into the earth chest-deep, as sure and true as a nail struck through a barrel.

I pushed and pulled at the hillside but there was no getting out of it. I had but one choice left.'

Jack took the rusted scythe blade and held it against his own throat.

The crowd shuddered.

'I cut my head clean off and sent it running home to fetch my Old Mother!'

Jack saw the Soldier, one hand upon the whetstone, the other fretting at the hilt of his sword.

'Are you calling me a liar, Sir?' asked Jack.

The Soldier stood sentry-straight but spoke not a word.

'Another man might, but not I,' said the Innkeeper. 'Tell on.'

'Well,' said Jack with a grin, 'my head went rolling down the hill quick, but not as quick as the fox from his den at the foot of it. Old Reynard got a sharp-toothed hold on me.'

Jack went to the Tinker's dog and made a show of the tussle against him with the mutton bone until the whole crowd were laughing.

Then Jack stopped and turned to them once more, solemn-eyed.

'Good folk, I know as well as the next man that the ending of this earthly road comes to all of us in time. But I'll tell you true: I will choose the manner of my departure and it will be a noble one.

'There's nothing like bold-blooded anger for the moving of a mountain.

I kicked my way out of that hillside and went running after.

I got hold of Old Reynard by the scruff of his neck and he dropped my pawed-upon pate in an instant.

But I wasn't about to let him go easy.

'I scolded him and shook him, and then, out his backside fell a litter of kits. Seven fine foxes, each no bigger than my fingertip.

Now that's no way for any beast to come into the world and these little fellows were that frit, they pissed where they were standing.

My poor head was that parched, with all its rolling and rattling, that before I could instruct it otherwise it was lapping up the foxes' water. And I'll tell you true, it had finer body to it than any ale that poured from the barrels of The Eagle and Child.'

'That is a barefaced lie!' cried the Innkeeper.

Jack bowed to his boots, grinning.

Then a shout came up from the back of the crowd.

'Enough!'

The field of folk parted like a sea as the Bishop of The Lands came striding through.

The Bishop tore the dressing from the well, staining his Holy slippers with the trampling of the blossoms. He ordered the Innkeeper to bring him a tumbler of whisky and a tumbler of water and set himself squarely between the Jack and the whetstone.

The Bishop placed the glasses upon the naked bricks, then knelt, scrabbling at the soil with the pecking purpose of a round-bellied robin. He came up triumphant with a wriggling worm caught fast between finger and thumb.

'Behold!' he thundered. 'This blind, crawling creature is more noble in its bearing and more beloved to Our Good Lord than any one of this company.'

He lowered the worm into the water glass, like the reverent resting of a relic. It turned and twisted against the casement.

The Innkeeper stepped forward but the Bishop brandished his brass-bound Bible before him like a shield.

'My tale will be told, Sir,' he said.

He pulled out a sheaf of parchment, took the side of the whetstone as his pulpit and spread his sermon out upon it.

'The Almighty provided a world of riches and wonder for you, his most beloved children. A land of milk and honey. But instead, you choose to drink the Devil's dram. Witness now the consequences.'

The Bishop plucked the worm from the water and doused it in the whisky glass. No sooner thus baptised, it ceased its wriggling and stilled upon the surface, its soul so swiftly departed.

'Eternal thanks, Your Worship!' cried out the Farmer's wife. 'My man's been run through with worms the last nine years; I'll be sure he takes the Devil's dose daily!'

The Innkeeper stepped forward but the Bishop held up his papal papers.

'Such ignorance of the allegorical is only to be expected,' he said. 'Therefore, let me present a more literal liturgy. The sermon of the **MALT**.'

The Holy Man gestured to the Mountebanks, with the peacock feathers now crowning their caps, gathered at the far side of the green where they had set a skittles stack of crab claws, rolling the pumpkin for the striking.

'Behold the Mercenary Men!' cried the Bishop. 'With claret-coddled consciousness, they turn the variety and wonder of God's own creations to Manipulation for pure profit.'

Then he gestured to the cluster of womenfolk gathered at the door of the inn, commandeering the use of the Merchant's pocketbook and pen for calculation as they emptied out the bitter and the bright contents of their aprons upon his table.

'Behold Eve's daughters!' cried the Bishop. 'Consumed by Appetite and Argument. How exaggerated these vices become, when assisted by the influence of Ale.'

The Tailor's sister and the Baker's wife matched the stern gaze of the Bishop with expressions of their own as they licked the salt and sugar from fingertip and thumb.

The Tinker's little dog snapped and snarled as the Bishop strode across the green and struck the flagon of ale from his master's hand.

'Shame on you, poor wretch, for your tawdry tradings,' cried the Bishop. 'Your tall tale is fashioned entirely from Licentiousness and Lunacy! Behold the truth of such corruption of body and mind – it is the savage justice of the Liquor.'

The Shepherd Boy held his gold guinea tight, with the edges set sharply between his knuckles as the Bishop approached.

'Your beer-boldened Blasphemy has brought you nothing but fool's gold, child,' cried the Bishop, shaking his scripture at the sky. 'The Torment of Hell is a Truth most Terrible and there are no worldly riches that can settle the debt upon your soul.'

In that moment, a savage screeching cut through the rhetoric.

There was Jack, standing by the whetstone, sharpening his scythe and whistling as he did so.

The Bishop was at his side in an instant, stilling the blade with one hand and grabbing the collar of Jack's coat with the other.

'Behold the serf of Satan, who tests the metal of tongue and blade alike, in the pursuit of profit for the purpose of pleasure,' cried the Bishop.

'Murder! Avarice! Lewdness! Trickery! Shame on you, Jack, who would claim a victory by stitching together all the worst of mankind's nature into nonsense, so that every vice might be laughed out of the conscience of the crowd. You speak of the nobility of your ending. I tell you, Sir, your Fate will be the very contrary. For you who tout a celebration of sin to line your own pockets with no care for the consequence upon the souls of your corrupted congregation, there will be no mercy. It will be upon a river of MALT that you depart from this world and there will be but one destination that awaits you – an eternity of Misery, Anguish, Lamentation and Torment.'

'Amen,' said Jack, as he raised his whisky glass, drank deeply and stepped away from his prize.

The Innkeeper strode forward.
    'Of all this fine company I do declare,' he cried, 'the Most Absolute Liar Therein and let none of you contest it.'

The many-headed crowd moved as one.
    The women stripped the Bishop of his robe and the men hauled up the whetstone and placed it inside, then set that pontifical package on the Holy Man's shoulders.

The Bishop stumbled through the applauding company, hunchbacked with the weight of his title, and was gone.

The Shepherd Boy's whistle sang out once more. The women plucked flower and fern from hedgerow and meadow and the well was redressed to full majesty: Marigold for luck, Sweet William for gratitude and Forget-Me-Not for fidelity. Whilst they worked away, Jack slipped a fistful of golden corn into the pocket of the Innkeeper.

So it was that the Malt flowed freely, and the misrule of May played out upon the village green until the sky turned and the swinging sign of the baby-bound bird was swallowed by the darkening night.

LITTLE STUPID

Once there was a widowed Merchant who lived in a house by the forest with his three daughters. The Eldest Daughter carried her beauty in her long golden hair, the Middle Daughter in her bright blue eyes. But they both held a dark-hearted ugliness within. The Youngest Daughter was beautiful both inside and out. Her sisters gave her the hard chores of the house, in the hope that the work would dull her loveliness. But whatever the task was – scrubbing the floors, digging the garden or chopping the firewood – she did it gladly and sung sweetly as she worked. The cruel sisters laughed at her good nature and called her Little Stupid.

When the time came for the Merchant to take the journey to the trading fair in the city at the heart of the Kingdom he called his Youngest Daughter to him and asked what trinket or treasure he might bring back for her.

Before Little Stupid could say a word, there was Golden Hair, pulling at her father's sleeve.

'Do I not patch the coat that keeps the chill from your bones as you walk the long roads? Does such kindness not deserve reward?'

The Merchant was not foolish. He had seen Golden Hair snatch the needle from Little Stupid and prick her milk-white skin with it, before taking his coat and claiming the neat, strong stitches as her own. But in truth, he was a little frightened of his Eldest Daughter and the cruelty of her hands. So he kissed her and he told her that she would have whatever her heart desired.

'Then I shall have a dress of golden silk to match my hair,' she said. 'So that the King of the Land will fall in love with me and I shall become Queen.'

Before the Merchant could say a word there was Blue Eyes pulling at his other sleeve.

'Do I not bake the sweet treats that fill the pockets of your coat and keep the hunger from your belly as you walk the long roads? Does such kindness not deserve reward?'

The Merchant was not foolish. He had seen Blue Eyes snatch the tray of honey cakes from Little Stupid and cast them across the floor at the sight of a burnt crust. But in truth, he was a little frightened of his Middle Daughter and the fierce fire of her temper. So he kissed her and he told her that she would have whatever her heart desired.

'Then I shall have a necklace of sapphires to match my eyes, so that the King of the Land will fall in love with me and I shall become Queen.'

'And you, my youngest?' said the Merchant with a smile. 'What will you do to win the heart of the King?'

Little Stupid smiled back in kind.

'If it pleases you, dear father, then I shall have a silver saucer and an apple made of glass.'

'Stupid is as Stupid does,' said Golden Hair.

The Merchant kissed his Little Stupid and told her that if it was truly what her heart desired then a glass apple and a silver saucer would be hers.

The days turned to weeks and the weeks to months. Golden Hair and Blue Eyes whiled away the time imagining how it would be to have the King's coffers of gold to spend as they wished and a castle full of servants to do their bidding. Meanwhile Little Stupid swept the house, harvested the garden and kept the hearth warm for her father's return.

By the time the Merchant came home the days were short and the nights dark, long and cold. Little Stupid welcomed her father, eased the coat from his shoulders and led him to his chair by the fire. Her older sisters went straight to his pack, scrabbling inside for their gifts, and they did not even stop to thank him for them.

That night, Golden Hair strutted back and forth in front of her mirror, delighting in the sumptuous shine of her silken dress.

Little Stupid sat beside the stove, rested the silver saucer on her lap, set the glass apple upon it and turned it widdershins, chasing time backwards. As it spun, there in the heart of the apple she saw the beginnings of the world and all that came after. She saw a four-pointed signpost quartering up a cloud-crested sky. She saw a Golden Bird circling a high mountain. She saw a cage crafted from the roots of an oak tree.

In the room next to her sister, Blue Eyes could not tear her gaze away from her own reflection, delighting in the shimmering sparkle of the precious stones set close around her throat.

The glass apple stilled upon the saucer. Little Stupid set her hand to it again and turned it as a watchmaker might wind a clock. As it spun, there in the heart of the apple she saw how the world might be lost or saved. She saw a Black Bull thundering down the long roads. She saw a coffin-caught Phoenix unfolding feathers of flame. She saw a tattered traveller shaking the fixings of the nine strong locks of Hell.

The following morning the older sisters found Little Stupid still sitting by the stove with the glass apple and silver saucer in her lap.

'Stupid is as Stupid does,' said Blue Eyes.

Little Stupid turned the apple first one way and then the other, twisting past and future together. The sisters watched over her shoulder as there in the heart of the apple the present world beyond their doorstep unfolded before them. There was the village, the towns, the long roads that led to a castle set high in the mountains and the handsome King sitting on his golden throne within that castle.

To Golden Hair, her dress now seemed dull. To Blue Eyes, the gemstones of her necklace lost their shine. The sisters' hearts were full of envy.

Little Stupid looked again into the apple and her heart was full of sorrow. Because there she saw her own death approaching, with sure and steady footsteps.

Little Stupid went to her father, who was counting the small coins he had left in his pockets, cursing the cost of gold silk and sapphires. She gave him the glass apple and the silver saucer and asked him to hold them in his safekeeping and to let no other man or woman lay a hand upon them until she returned. His mind was so full of commonplace calculation that he did not think to question her request.

The cruel sisters were waiting for her at the doorstep, and they were carrying large cloth-covered baskets.

'Come, dear sister,' said Golden Hair, 'let us gather blackberries together.'

She took one arm, Blue Eyes took the other, and together they led Little Stupid into the forest.

The bare branches of the trees twisted upwards above their heads, like bony fingers clawing at the sky. By the side of the winding paths the blackberries shone jewel bright, but whenever Little Stupid paused to pick them, the sisters pulled her onwards.

'The sweetest fruits grow furthest in,' said Blue Eyes.

The paths ahead grew tangled as if the woods were weaving themselves together to block their way. They reached a clearing amidst a ring of birch trees. The earth beneath was damp and dark and no birds sang.

The older sisters set down their baskets and drew back the cloths. There was the sharp-pointed spade and the keen-bladed woodaxe.

The night was fully fallen when Golden Hair and Blue Eyes returned home. Their dresses were torn, their faces blackened with dirt and they wept as they told their father how Little Stupid had proved the truth of her name. How she was so caught up in her daydreams that she had wandered from them, and they had searched and searched but they could not find her. And now the night was full of the howling of wolves at the hunt.

Their father held them close and wept alongside them.

'It would give me great comfort,' said Golden Hair, 'if I might have that silver saucer by which to remember my dear sister.'

'And it would comfort me also,' said Blue Eyes, 'if I might have the glass apple to look upon and think of her.'

Then the Merchant remembered Little Stupid's last words to him. He put the glass apple and the silver saucer into a strong box, locked it and placed the key on a chain around his neck.

The Merchant may have wished the world to cease turning after the loss of Little Stupid, but it did not.

One morning the following Spring, a Shepherd Boy named Ivan was tending his flock in the fields at the other side of the forest. An eager and skittish lamb jumped the fence and disappeared into the undergrowth. Ivan followed, and as he ran down those twisting paths a sound came calling to him across the breeze. A sound that was part birdsong, part laughter.

He followed it deep into the heart of the forest, where he came to a ring of birch trees. At the centre of the clearing there was a mound of earth covered with purple flowers. Ivan was a boy of the farm and the fields, and he saw those bright blooms for what they were – Honesty of the woodland.

Perching on a hawthorn bush beside was a small brown wren, singing out her song to the sunlight. As Ivan stood and listened to the sweet melody he heard a woman's voice, softly echoing the bird note for note. He drew closer to the mound of earth and there he saw, standing straight and true in the heart of the Honesty, a single reed and it was singing.

Ivan thought of the travelling men who brought the fair to the village green at high Summer, and how they would play tunes on their wooden whistles and how their caps would fill with coins. He thought how this would be a merrier way of making a living than the weary work of a shepherd. And merrier still if he did not have to go to the trouble of mastering an instrument. So he took out his pocketknife, cut the reed and carved it accordingly.

No sooner was this done than the reed-whistle began to sing.

'Play, little pipe, play.
Play sweet sorrows to the clear blue sky.
Songs to comfort my poor dear father,
Who knows not where in the woods I lie.'

Ivan saw then the true nature of that mound of earth and he ran, as fast as he could away from the forest, the loss of his soul a greater fear for him than the loss of a lamb. He buried the reed deep in his pocket but that sweet voice, so soft and yet so strong, only sang louder and louder.

By the evening of that same day, all the villagers had come out to the lambing field to witness the strange enchantment. The Merchant was amongst them and when he heard the voice of his dear lost daughter calling to him, he pushed through the crowds.

He grabbed the reed in one hand, the other he placed around Ivan's throat.

Then the reed-whistle changed its song.

'Play little pipe, play.
Play sweet sorrows to the evening air.
Songs to comfort my poor dear father,
And to lead him to his daughter fair.'

Ivan took the Merchant to the birch-bound clearing and together they dug as the night grew dark around them. There, beneath the Honesty, beneath the dark clods of earth, they found Little Stupid. There was no sign of the harm that had been done to her. Her skin was milk-white, her ruby-red lips held the shadow of a smile. Her eyes were closed; she seemed as though she were sleeping. The Merchant pulled her from the grave, held her close, kissed her a hundred times over but she did not stir.

Then the reed-whistle changed its song once more.

'Oh poor dear father, do not forsake me.
Fetch water from the Royal Well to wake me.
'Til then, hidden let my body be,
Guarded by the broad birch tree.'

The Merchant was not foolish. Although it broke his heart to place his most-loved daughter back beneath the earth, he did as the enchanted whistle instructed. Upon his return home, he spoke not a word of these events to Golden Hair and Blue Eyes. The very next morning he put his pack upon his back and set out. He gave Ivan a purse of silver coins in exchange for a promise to guard that birch tree grove day and night until he returned.

It was a long and treacherous road that led from the house by the forest to the castle of the King. But this is the tale of Little Stupid, so her father's courage and cunning on that journey full of danger and wonder must be told in other stories.

So it was that after a year and a day the Merchant came to the grand castle high in the mountains, where the King sat upon his golden throne in the great chamber.

The Merchant knelt before him, offering up all the treasures in his pack in return for a few drops of water from the Royal Well.

The King looked down upon him with a gaze that was full of sorrow.

'What need have I of a Merchant's trinkets,' he said, 'when I have all the riches of the world?'

'Then what might I provide, my Lord and Emperor,' replied the Merchant, 'so that I may gain your favour?'

'Company,' said the King. 'And a good story.'

That night the Merchant and the King feasted together in his private chambers and the Merchant told his tale. He told of the death of his dear wife, of his three daughters – the one that he loved and the two that he feared. He told of the singing reed-whistle and the grave of Honesty. He told of the glass apple and the silver saucer and the key on the chain that he wore around his neck.

Then the King ordered his manservant to draw water from the Royal Well and to stopper it up in a bottle made of blue glass. He ordered his groomsman to fix four strong black horses to his golden carriage. He ordered the Merchant to ride as fast as hooves and wheels could carry him and to hasten back with the glass apple and the silver saucer and all three of his daughters.

The road that was long on the setting out was short on the return. The villagers watched with wonder as the Merchant rode that golden carriage into the square, tied up the majestic steeds and went running into the forest, as if he had the Devil at his heels.

There in the birch clearing was the grave with faithful Ivan sitting beside it, playing on the reed-whistle. Together they turned the soil once more and there was Little Stupid, still smiling in her sleep. No sooner had the Merchant placed a drop of the water from the Royal Well upon her lips than she opened her eyes. There were tears and kisses, and there was another purse of silver coins for Ivan.

When Golden Hair and Blue Eyes saw the Royal carriage riding up to the house, they ran to fetch their silk dress and their sapphire necklace, and they pinched and pushed each other as they squabbled about who would be Queen of the Land and who would not.

When they saw Little Stupid and their father climb down from that carriage they began to tremble and weep. But they disguised their fear as joy at the return of their lost sister. Little Stupid smiled and matched their kisses with kisses of her own. Then she unlocked her father's strong box and held on tightly to her glass apple and her silver saucer as they all rode back to the castle together.

The moment the King set eyes upon Little Stupid his loneliness lifted from his heart. She knelt before him and in return for the life that he had given back to her, she offered up to him the things as precious to her as life itself – her glass apple and her silver saucer.

There at the foot of the golden throne in the great chamber, she turned the eye of the apple to the past and she spun it.

In the heart of the twisting glass was the forest and the ring of birch trees and the three sisters and the axe that cut and the spade that dug and the dark clods of earth that came tumbling after.

The Merchant wept and the King flew into a terrible rage. He called upon his guardsmen to bind Golden Hair and Blue Eyes hand and foot and for them to be locked in the dark dungeon in the depths of the castle.

But Little Stupid stayed his hand.

'Stupid is as Stupid does,' she said. 'Let not malice blind the merciful.'

The King was moved by her words and he pardoned Golden Hair and Blue Eyes for their wickedness. Although whether they ever found forgiveness from their own father I do not know.

Little Stupid became Queen of the Land, and a silver throne was set beside the gold one. There she would sit, spinning her glass apple in her silver saucer and offering kind counsel and guidance to her husband over all matters of the Kingdom. Their reign was long and prosperous and peaceful.

When Ivan the Shepherd Boy heard of the marriage he put the reed-whistle back into his pocket and set out for the Kingdoms Beyond. Many travellers on the long roads still speak today of the old tinker and his magic whistle and at night they sing his songs by the fireside. Songs about a love that was found buried deep in a birch grove and lost on the road to fortune.

LITTLE DOG TURPIE

Once there was a Little Girl who lived with an Old Man and an Old Woman in a house made of hempstalks. How she came to be there, I do not know. She had no understanding of herself or any recollection of another life than the one she woke into each and every day.

Beyond the house there was a wide green field of hemp. Each morning the Old Man took up his sharp scythe and went out to harvest. The Old Woman would then set stone to stalk, pummelling out the pith.

The Little Girl was given the work that she was told small hands are made for – the teasing out, the spinning and the twisting. Every day the Old Man gave the same instruction. 'Seven spun skeins before slumber, Little Girl, or the worse it will go for you.'

The Old Man and his wife would set out to the alehouse and return reeling to bed whilst the Little Girl sat upon the doorstep and spun by starlight, filling the skein sack at her feet.

Her only company and her only friend was Little Dog Turpie, as faithful as his master was cruel. He would hunker down beside, watchful, until the work was done.

One Midsummer's Eve there they both were, spinning and stargazing, when across the warm breeze there came a whisper.

'Hobyah! Hobyah! Hobyah!
Tear down the hempstalks.
Eat up the Old Man and Woman
And carry off the Little Girl!'

She looked down at her hands, so bloodied and blighted by the roughness of the work. She looked at the stack of hewn hemp upon the doorstep, still unspun. She looked at the hut, with its tightly woven walls. She thought of what it might mean to be carried away from all of it, of what great adventures she and Little Dog Turpie might have together in the wide world beyond.

She stood and cried out to the night, words stolen from her own cruel master.

'Tittle tattle, tongues do rattle.
Fetch and fettle, prove your mettle!'

No sooner had she spoken than Little Dog Turpie leapt from the step and went racing out to the edge of the hemp field, barking and biting at the air as if he meant to chew up the night itself.

The door of the hempstalk house flung open and there was the Old Man, raging.

'Little Dog Turpie barks so that I cannot sleep nor slumber,' he cried. 'If I live till morning I will have his tail.'

At dawn the Old Woman came out, with her husband beside her. She caught Little Dog Turpie by the scruff of the neck and held him down as the Old Man scythed away. The tail was cut clean off and flung fieldwards. The Little Girl watched on, weeping.

Then the day went the way that it always did. The harvest, the stone-striking then the alehouse for the Old Man and his wife, the doorstep and the spinning for the Little Girl.

But she could not settle. With every twist of the long-dropping thread all she could see was a torn-away tail, twitching in her hand.

Little Dog Turpie sat beside her silent, staring out.

As the night came creeping in so did the weaving whispers, rippling and rustling through the field as if the leaves of the hemp had grown a voice.

'Hobyah! Hobyah! Hobyah!
Tear down the hempstalks.
Eat up the Old Man and Woman
And carry off the Little Girl!'

Little Dog Turpie reared up, snapping and snarling.

The Little Girl may have wished for a life beyond the one she was so stuck within, but she loved Little Dog Turpie more – and she knew full well now the cost of his boundary barking. So she stood strong and cried out to the night, again using words stolen from her cruel master.

'Still your tongue and cease your cries.
Or I'll have my dog eat you alive!'

But she was too late. The Old Man was raging at the doorstep once more.

'Little Dog Turpie barks so that I cannot sleep nor slumber,' he cried. 'If I live till morning I will have his legs.'

At dawn Little Dog Turpie scrabbled and scratched against the grip of the Old Woman as she had him up onto the step and knelt upon his back. Her husband swung the scythe and took the legs out from under him, one by one – flinging them to the field and laughing as he did so.

The Little Girl cradled Little Dog Turpie to her and wept. Her salt tears fell upon his severed stumps and stopped the bleeding. She wrapped him in her apron, tucked him tight and close inside her coat.

When the Old Man and his wife came stumbling home she had spun but one skein out of the seven.

Twilight settled on the hempfield, turning the green leaves to grey as if their very sap-blood was leaching away. Behind the fading of the quick colour, the whispers came once more.

'Hobyah! Hobyah! Hobyah!
Tear down the hempstalks.
Eat up the Old Man and Woman
And carry off the Little Girl!'

Her close-fastened coat could not contain Little Dog Turpie's keening. He howled fit to shatter the sky.

The Old Man came out shaking his scythe, with his wife following directly on his heels.

'Little Dog Turpie barks so that I cannot sleep nor slumber,' he raged. 'He shall not live till morning, for I will have his head.'

The Old Woman took Little Dog Turpie, put her foot upon him, holding his jaws tight shut as her husband brought the blade down quick, then kicked the head into the high hemp.

The night stood silent for a moment.
    Then it did not.

'Hobyah! Hobyah! Hobyah!
Tear down the hempstalks.
Eat up the Old Man and Woman
And carry off the Little Girl!'

The song sang out like a call to battle.

The ground beneath their feet shook and the stalks went spinning skywards as out came the Hobyahs.

Ink-black imps, tadpole-tailed, fish-eyed, with fists and feet built for breaking.

The wide field was torn and trampled, the hempstalk house followed. The Old Man and the Old Woman were swiftly slaughtered and swallowed.

The Little Girl was bound hand and foot and bundled into the skein sack.

The Hobyahs rode that sack across the razed land – one hauling at the drawstring, two at the head of the bag, one at the foot of it and one perched on top, crowing.

What manner of home the Hobyahs dwelt in I do not know, but this was the place where the Little Girl was taken. They hung that sack upon a high hook and cavorted about it, kicking at the cloth and crying out in glee.

'Look me! Look me!'

Inside the bag, the Little Girl wept.

She wept for the stealing of her cruel master's words that had called the creatures across the boundary of field and farm. She wept for the loss of her Little Dog Turpie. But she smiled as she thought of the Old Man and the Old Woman, and how their bones had cracked and crunched and how quickly they had been licked clean. The more she thought on this, the more something deep inside her twisted and blackened.

As dawn came, the Hobyahs nestled into one another like a ball of tightly wrapped twine, and rolled into the darkest corner of the room. There they slept, whilst the sack-stuck Little Girl swung back and forth on the hook above them.

Over the far horizon of the land that had once been hempfield there was a long road and walking along that road was a Tinker, with a black bag slung across his shoulder. He gazed out across the desolate dirtscape, and he saw the semblance of a path cut down the middle of it – a rut of well-trodden earth, marked out by scampering footprints.

'Well, where there's tracks, there's treasure,' he said.

The Tinker followed the way of the Hobyahs.

As the path ran on, he found, scattered at the side of it, dog tail, legs, body and head. He gathered them up carefully and placed them inside his black bag.

At the end of the path, he found set into the earth a single stone doorstep.

Beyond this threshold to nowhere he saw, cast aside like spillikins, a stack of bones, crowned with two grinning skulls.

He set his black bag down upon the doorstep, and no sooner had he done so than it began to writhe and wriggle.

Then there was a bold bark.

The Tinker loosened the drawstring and out there came head, body, legs and wagging tail.

No sooner had Little Dog Turpie tumbled back into life, he set his snout to the soil and was off – with the Tinker close behind him.

Little Dog Turpie followed the sour sack-dragged scent of Fear until he came to the home of the Hobyahs. The Tinker drew a pin from his pocket and unpicked the lock of the strong door.

There he found the Little Girl swinging in the sack and he set her free. She laughed and wept as Little Dog Turpie jumped up to meet her.

The Tinker told his half of the story. Then the Little Girl told hers in small whispers, pointing to the corner where the curled cluster of Hobyahs slept on.

'There's only one right way of reckoning,' said the Tinker. 'Like for like and without any measure of mercy.'

He held open the strewn-aside skein sack and Little Dog Turpie jumped straight in.

The Tinker and the Little Girl stood behind the strong door and they waited.

As twilight came the Little Girl crouched at the keyhole and whispered.

'Hobyah! Hobyah! Hobyah!
You tore down the hempstalks.
Ate up the Old Man and Woman
Now look thee to the Little Girl!'

That tangle of twisted Hobyahs unravelled and the five fierce fellows shook aside sleep and slumber and ran to the swinging sack.

They cackled as they clambered upon one another's shoulders for the unhooking.

One tipped up the foot, two hoisted the head of it and they laid it down upon the floor between them.

One pulled at the drawstring, another perched on top, punching and poking and crying out,

'Look me! Look me!'

Out came Little Dog Turpie, barking, biting, snapping and snarling, and he gobbled up the Hobyahs, each and every one.

And that is why there are no Hobyahs any more.

So it was that the Little Girl, the Tinker and Little Dog Turpie turned their backs on the barren field, the stone step and the pile of bones beside it and set out together on the long roads.

Whether that twisted blackness that blighted the Little Girl released its hold on her, or whether she grew more Hobyah-hearted as the years passed, is a tale to be told in another story.

THE ROOTS OF FORTUNE

O nce there was a Pedlar who lived in a village in the East of the land and his name was John Chapman. Whether it was down to bad luck or bad company I do not know, but it always went the same way for poor John. He would fill his pack in one town, empty it in another, with only ever a few pennies left for profit.

Each time he trudged home, it seemed to him that his cottage was sinking by sure and steady inches back into the ground it stood upon. He gained no solace from the sweet songs of the warbler, songthrush, blackbird and woodlark nesting in the rotting rafters of the rooftop, rather their joy at each new day seemed a mockery of his misery. He saw no beauty or purpose in the new green growth of the oak tree in his garden. For what was the use in an acorn harvest without the hogs to feed upon it? John's only comfort was his faithful dog who never strayed beyond his heels, day or night.

So it was, one warm Spring evening, John was laid out on his straw mattress with his dog beside him when a soft voice came whispering into his dreams.

'Arise, John Chapman, go swift and go with care
To London Bridge, and find your fortune there.'

He woke. The wind was whistling through the weathered wall at his back. His dog slept on regardless.

John thought of how the loss of a living was nothing when set against the loss of a man's wits.

He pulled his cap tight over his ears, set his cheek to his rag pillow and screwed his eyes tight shut.

The following morning John scraped moss from the bark of his oak tree and stoppered up the gaps between the wattle and the wood of the walls.

But when night fell and sleep came that voice called into his dreams once more, clear and commanding.

'Arise, John Chapman, go swift and go with care
To London Bridge, and find your fortune there.'

He woke. At his feet, his dog was scrabbling and scratching, as if running rat-catching through his own dream. Before him, the cottage door had dropped on its one good hinge and was striking against the sill.

John thought of how the loss of sense set aside the loss of wits was the worst poverty any man could suffer.

He pulled his cap down tight, placed his rag pillow over his head, shut his eyes and once more turned his back against the tricks of the night.

The following morning John cut a stout branch from that oak tree and fashioned it into a doorstop.

But when night and sleep returned, so did the voice, strong and stern.

*'Arise, John Chapman, go swift and go with care
To London Bridge, and find your fortune there.'*

He woke. His dog jumped up beside him, barking out into the night. The stars winked down at him through the rafters, like scattered silver.

John thought of how a man might wrestle with his wits, sharpen his senses and follow his dreams accordingly.

So he set out, with his dog at his heels.

The journey turned this way and that against John, as it always did.

By the time he met the Great North Road, he had an empty pack and a single shilling in his pocket. After he passed through the toll at the boundary of the city, he had but one penny left to his name.

London Bridge stretched out before him, unlike any other bridge he had ever set foot upon.

The wide water it spanned seemed more lake than river. There was a multitude of proud-masted ships crowded at the crossing, the sailor lads souring the air with their curses as they chartered their course.

Then there was the world above the water.

Tall-timbered tradehouses lined both sides of the road ahead. There were the trades John knew – the bakers, bookmakers, ironmongers, innkeepers, tailors, tanners, the millers and the merchants.

Then sat shoulder to shoulder amongst them were the trades that were unfamiliar to him. There was a painted and perfumed lady, stood in the darkened doorway of a house, casting kisses to the wind. There was a sallow-skinned man dressed in silk, leaning out from a window of a house opposite with a chattering monkey perched upon his shoulder, beckoning. There was a boy balancing on the gutter's edge, tumbling head over heels, plucking doves from his pockets and throwing them skywards.

Then there was the press of folk before and behind him, the drovers and the drunkards, the paupers and the pilgrims, the soldiers and the showmen. An echo of the churning of the brown waters of the Thames, a great stinking swell of humanity ready to uproot him from the spot he stood upon and set to tip him beneath the wheels of the carts and the carriages that thundered down the run of the road ahead.

His mind reeled against the impossibility of this place – and also against the seemingly impossible purpose that he had dreamt for himself within it.

Nevertheless, he called himself to courage. With his dog chasing at his heels, he shouldered his way through the many-headed crowd until he was at the centre of that bustling bridge. There he stood, sentry-still, watching and waiting.

It was not long before the men came plucking at his pack and his pockets. A weather-faced old rogue, holding out a weighted double-headed dice that would always fall in his own favour. A tatter-clad young man, presenting a claw-hooked key that would slip any lock in Christendom. A small, thin shadow of a lad, whispering the wonders of the wineskin he pulled from beneath his belt, of how one sip would set any enemy into a slumber that would never be broken.

But John Chapman was as honest as he was unlucky, and he turned his back upon each and every false fortune that was offered up to him. He kept his single penny clutched tight in his fist and when the sky turned twilight and the shop doors were bolted and the shutters were drawn, he made his way to the bank of clay beneath the bridge, laid out his pack for a blanket, pulled his coat tight around him and set himself down to sleep. His dog sat at his feet, faithful and watchful. When John's dreams came, they were misted and uncertain, and held neither encouragement nor instruction.

He woke with the dawn, and with a hunger roiling in his belly, returned to the world above.

He thought upon the many winding ways of fortune-seeking and how a man rarely got rich by standing still upon one spot.

So John Chapman spent his second day roaming London Bridge, back and forth, forth and back, until his boots were breaking.

It was the women who came calling that day, pulling at his sleeve and shoulder. A crooked-toothed crone, holding out a shattered scrying glass and attesting to the truth of its reflections. A maiden with a voice as bold as her brassy yellow hair, presenting a potion of herbs and honey that promised both love and forgetting. A barefooted slip of a lass, whispering the wonders of her magic black bag that would fix any broken article placed inside it.

Luckless but noble John Chapman held tight to his principles and to that one last penny and he turned his back on all of it.

Once again, he slept on that cold clay embankment, with his dog sat sentry beside him. Once again, his shadowed, shifting dreams brought neither solace nor solution.

At dawn of the third day, John found himself back upon the bridge. Before him there was the clattering chaos of the street. Behind him, there was the road he had taken.

He took the penny from his pocket, examined the head and the tail of it and was just about to set the compass of his life accordingly when he felt a hand upon his back. He turned. There stood before him was a smiling Gentleman.

'My friend,' said the Gentleman. 'May I trouble you with a question?'

'Most certainly,' said John, who although both heartsore and footsore still matched the Gentleman's smile with his own. 'However, it has come to my attention that I am not blessed with any natural abilities of understanding or deduction.'

The Gentleman regarded John for a moment and then when he spoke, he did so softly, and with kindness.

'I confess, you have kindled my curiosity. I have watched your progress across the bridge these past few days. Do you have no wares to sell?'

'That I do not,' replied John.

'And yet you have not set yourself up as a beggar?'

John felt the rough ridges of the penny in his pocket.

'Not whilst I have my own coin to keep me,' he replied.

'Then what possible purpose can there be in such entirely fruitless standing?'

John set his gaze upon the Gentleman's fine polished boots as he told the tale of his thrice-repeated dream and of how the words that began as a whisper had gathered to the urgency of an order and how the following of that order had led to his present predicament.

The Gentleman threw back his head and laughed so loud that he startled the flock of a passing gooseherd. As the boy beat the birds back into formation, their honking and hollering seemed to John a cackling chorus at his own folly and he felt his cheeks burning with the shame of it.

'My dear country-voiced fellow,' said the Gentleman, 'such night visions are the Devil's own deceptions cast upon our conscience to test us. Why, only last night I dreamt of a squalid little shack, broken-beamed, with walls open to the weather. Beside it stood a tall oak, mottled with moss. And as I gazed upon that tree the earth beneath turned itself aside and revealed, resting in the rootstock, a great pot of treasure.'

John Chapman stood still and silent. At his feet beside him, his dog pricked up his ears.

'Imagine the ruination of my good reputation,' continued the Gentleman, 'if I were to set out on the long roads in pursuit of such a fictitious fortune. Learn wit from a wiser man than thyself, my friend. Return and set your full attention to the practical world before you. Place no further favour upon your fancies.'

John understood then the exact direction of his dreams.

He bowed before the Gentleman and thanked him for his kind counsel. Then he turned his back upon London Bridge, this world set betwixt land, air and water, and he walked on. A road taken with certainty and purpose runs more swiftly than one taken with caution. It was not long before 101 miles were behind John Chapman, and he was back at the threshold of his cottage.

He wrenched the slipped door from its hinges in his eagerness, took the rusted coal shovel from his hearth and down he dug, with his dog scrabbling at the soil beside him.

There was the run of the rootstock. And there, nestled in amongst it as if the tree itself was holding the treasure in its twig-twisted embrace, was a pot fashioned from red clay.

John inched it out. He wiped it down clean. There was an inscription running around the belly of it.

SUB QUO HOC POSITUM EST
ALIUD MELIUS QUAM EGO REQUIESCIT

John knew this to be church language, but the meaning of the words was beyond him. Nevertheless, he bowed his head, offering up a prayer of thanks to The Almighty. Then he unstoppered the lid of that pot and upended it.

The silver coins chimed and chattered as they fell. They filled John's pockets to bursting.

The next morning John went to market whistling. He bought new boots, a long fine coat with sturdy pockets sewn both inside and out. He told any man who would listen of how the tales were true – the road to London was indeed the road to fortune. But he did not share the exact nature by which his luck had turned.

He pressed silver into the palms of the craftsmen – the Woodcutter, the Thatcher and the Blacksmith. Before the week was out, the walls of his home stood straight and true. The roof was sealed up tight and he had a strong oak door, set with bright brass hinges and sturdy lock, with the key to fit it.

John and his dog sat by their fireside, content. John had a belly full of mutton stew, and his faithful companion was wrestling with the bone.

But when he took to his fine feather bed, John found that he could not settle.

His mind was troubled by the instructions held in words that he could not comprehend.

As dawn broke, John found himself copying out the inscription in a careful hand.

SUB QUO HOC POSITUM EST
ALIUD MELIUS QUAM EGO REQUIESCIT

Then he set out, with his dog beside him.

John found the Priest of the village standing in the nave of his church, frowning up at the Heavens – slices of a sullen sky running between the rafters. Pails and pans processed down the aisle before him, the rooftop rainfall striking out a symphony.

'Honest John Chapman,' said the Priest. 'Well met indeed. For it is my intention to set you in my Sunday Sermon. A living parable of how The Almighty favours the pure-minded and patient man.'

John gave thanks once more as he cast a pocketful of silver onto the collection plate. Then, under the kindly gaze of the Holy Man he gave his true confession. The Priest clapped his hands in delight.

'I have heard tales of times past concerning such angelic visitation, but never have I encountered such incontrovertible evidence,' he said. 'Pray, tell on, Honest John, and tell true.'

So John told of London Bridge and all that he had encountered there. He told of the treasure dug from his own land and the words that came with it.

The Priest studied John's scrawled script and smiled once more.

'It appears you are twice blessed, my child,' he said. 'The translation is both simple and certain.'

The Priest spoke the words with the soft reverence of a prayer.

> *BENEATH WHERE THIS DOES LIE*
> *RESTS ANOTHER, FAR BETTER THAN I.*

John understood the wider truth of the message then, and he spoke it out clearly.

'A blessing perhaps,' he said. 'But one that my own ignorance would have blinded me to, Sir, without your kind counsel.'

The Heavens held back the rainfall as Priest and Pedlar knelt side by side, one with the borrowed trowel of the gravedigger in his hand, the other with the coal shovel, as they burrowed deep into those roots of fortune until the air rang with the sound of metal meeting stone.

The ochre-coloured urn took both the men's strength to lift and when they upended it, the golden coins that tumbled out stacked up to their ankles.

The dog ran rings around the treasure trove, barking out his delight.

The Priest rubbed cloth against clay and there was more Latin lettering. John peered down at the pot and spelt out the words as he saw them.

ADVENA, QUID PRODEST OMNE AURUM
SAECULI HABERE
CUM FUGIANT AVIDO MENS ANIMUSQUE TIBI

As John spoke he felt a coldness come crawling through his blood. As if he was calling something not entirely of this world into being.

'Indeed, Honest John, indeed,' said the Priest. 'This wealth carries a warning that any man would do well to take heed of.'

He crossed himself then spoke out the meaning with the soft certainty of scripture.

WHAT USE TO MAN IS WORLDLY GOLD
IF THE GETTING OF IT COSTS HIM HIS SOUL?

John Chapman returned to market once more, with the Priest at his side. Together they brokered and bargained with stonemasons, the master woodworkers and the men practised in the art of the staining and setting of glass.

The church of that village still stands to this day – sure and steady and true.

And Honest John Chapman the Pedlar can still be found within it. There, set upon an oaken pew post, the height of a handspan, with his pack upon his back, forever striding out to find his fortune. His dog sits beside him, post-bound at his side and forever faithful.

The London folk are also there, if you know how to look for them. Transformed by sleight of hand and the gaze of God, the bawdy woman of the dark doorways now stands penitent and mild, rosary in hand. The magician gazes from his window, serene and still, untroubled by any monkey mischief.

But the greatest wonder is the transformation of the rooftops.

An abundant choir of angels roosts in the rafters, immortal and triumphant, gazing down upon the world below, their wooden eyes unblinking.

Some folk say that the honest Pedlar crafted the Angels of Fortune in eternal thanks for their visitation and their favour.

Other folk say that it was the Devil himself who tempted the foolish traveller with a cache of cursed coin. They say that John Chapman set the angels upon the eaves in the hope that when his time came, they might show mercy and haul him up to the Heavens, away from the Fate and the Fire that was surely his due.

JOHNNIE-HE-NOT

Once there was a Farmer's wife and her name was Tibbie. She had her own particular way of looking at the world, paying more attention to what was lacking in her life than to the counting of her blessings. Her husband was a man of work rather than words and he had little time for her complaints.

Whilst the Farmer tended his land and his livestock, Tibbie sat alone at the kitchen hearth. She whispered her longings to the flickering flames, of how she would give all that she had in return for the one thing she had not – a child.

As the coals shifted against the grate and sighed in sympathy, someone or something heard her.

Springtime came. The forest, fields and farmstead were all burgeoning and blossoming with new life and so was Tibbie. She laughed at the lambing, cried at the calving and by the time Harvest rolled round her belly was drum-tight.

Her boy was born with eyes the colour of chestnuts, skin as soft as butter and his hair was coppice-copper bright. He was well loved by both his mother and his father, and they named him Johnnie.

Johnnie was simple to suckle and swift to sleep. Nevertheless, Tibbie would be awake half the night, cooing over the cradle, marvelling at the miracle of him.

One morning, her husband already out with the dawn and at the plough, Tibbie came to the barn to find the water trough upended and the calves leaping across it for their sport. The cobbles were slick and slippery. Johnnie was hugging at her hip, unbalancing her at every step.

Tibbie went to the kitchen, drew up the fireguard and set Johnnie down in the cradle. She kissed him and tucked him in tight.

'You'll not even have breath for blinking before I'm back,' she said.

Tibbie ran a swift rope as she hauled the pails from the well and set the yoke about her neck. She was at the trough in an instant, then round the midden and the peat stack and heading for the cottage.

She was crossing the yard when she heard it. A savage screeching like the sticking of the sow at slaughter. Except that this was harder, harsher, and human.

Tibbie all but ripped the kitchen door from the hinges as she went flying through it.

She grabbed Johnnie from the cradle. His face was plum-puce, his smock sodden with salt tears. He beat his fists against her breast and there was nothing she could do or say to bring him comfort.

From that day onwards, it always went the same.

Johnnie would be all sweetness and smiles at dawn. But as soon as the Farmer set out for work, then Johnnie would be racketing and rioting, and not cease until dusk fell and his father returned.

Tibbie's skin bloomed black and blue with all his punching and pinching. Her milk soured and then ceased. But she knew well enough this was fair dues for desertion. So she bore her shame in secret and spoke of it to no one.

There are secrets that need to be spoken and then there are those that travel swiftly on a strong wind.

Beyond the farmyard there was a road, and in a cottage on the other side of that road lived a Tailor. His name was Old Wullie. He was a quiet and careful man, with wits as nimble as his fingers. He knew that when folk came to him with a coat slashed at chest and pocket or a dress torn at bodice and hem, it's fair costing not questions they're after.

Old Wullie stoppered up his ears with cotton, stuffed salvages of velvet into the lintels of the window, but the howling leaked through regardless. It frayed his nerves until every seam he set ran crooked.

He could feel his fortune slipping through his fingers, alongside his reputation. One morning he could bear it no longer. So, he put his pack upon his back, grabbed a fistful of buttons and ribbons and went knocking at Tibbie's kitchen door.

When Tibbie saw Old Wullie offering up his trinkets, she thought how long it was since there had been any kind of brightness or beauty in her life. She swallowed back her shame and welcomed him in.

'Don't mind our wee Johnnie,' she said, with a voice as brittle as her smile. 'These daft turns of his soon blow over.'

Old Wullie looked at the bawling babe that was twisting against her embrace. 'There's many kinds of words for the likes of him,' he said, 'but Johnnie he not.'

Tibbie recalled the tales she had heard about her good neighbour, the wise Tailor whose trust was as strong and tight as his stitches.

'Then what name would you give him?' she asked in a whisper.

'Less said, soonest mended,' said Old Wullie as he drew a chair up close to the fire. 'But I'll tell you true, there are three roads you can take to the reckoning of this matter. I'm in mind to start with the one most trodden.'

Old Wullie undid his pack and took out a bunch of hops and barley, a fresh egg and a silver needle. Then he turned and looked at Tibbie directly.

'You get yourself the other side of that strong door, girl, lock it tight. And whatever you see or hear, don't move an inch until the supper's swallowed.'

Tibbie did as she was told. Then she pressed her cheek to the rough wood and set her eye to the keyhole.

She watched as Old Wullie pierced the eggshell with the needle and set his mouth to it. He sucked until his cheeks were full then spat into the hearth. Then he cracked the blown egg clean in two.

He took water from the jug and poured it into the half that had no hole. He crushed the hops and barley between finger and thumb and placed them in the water. He set the frail flagon in the ashes of the fire and waited.

There crawling along the lip of the cradle came a withered hand. Peeking out behind it, small squinting eyes as black as coal.

Tibbie crammed her apron into her mouth to stopper up her screaming and she watched on.

Johnnie-He-Not pulled himself up to full standing, folded bony arms about his buckled belly and he grinned. His smile stretched across his leathery face from the tip of one ear to the other.

When he spoke, it was with a voice that tore the air.

'I am old, older than old,' he cried. 'But never in my livelong life have I ever seen a Tailor mash beer in an eggshell.'

Johnnie-He-Not leapt down from the cradle, grabbed the egg from the hearth and swallowed it whole.

'More!' he cried. 'And stronger!'

Then he let out a great whoop and went diving back down into his blankets.

When Tibbie could bring herself to cross the threshold and look down into the cradle, there was the semblance of her son, squalling in his sleep.

'Fret not,' said Old Wullie. 'One road's taken, there's two left for the walking.'

Then he shouldered his pack onto his back and bade her good night.

When the Farmer returned, Tibbie took him out to the coal shed and wept as she told how she had favoured the care of the cattle over the care of their child and all that had come after. She told of the wisdom of their good neighbour and how if they stood together on this matter, they might find a way to fix it.

As Tibbie spoke she felt the great gaping silence between herself and her husband grow darker and wider. When there was no more to be told, the Farmer turned and set out across the fields without as much as a backwards glance.

The thing in the cradle howled the whole night through. Although it bore the face and form of her Johnnie, Tibbie could not bring herself to touch it.

Dawn was breaking when Old Wullie came knocking for the second time.

'You get this side and I'll get that,' said the Tailor, swinging the door shut between them. 'And whatever you see or hear, don't move an inch until the dram is drunk.'

Tibbie spied silently as Old Wullie drew the chair close to the fire and took his pack from his back. She felt a shifting in the air beside her. She turned – there was her husband. She put her finger to his lips and guided his gaze to the crack at the hinge of the strong door.

The moment Old Wullie had the whisky out, Johnnie-He-Not came rearing up from the cradle, grabbing at the bottle. His twisted mouth gaped open wide, and he swallowed it all down in one gulp.

'More!' he cried. 'And stronger!'

Then he let out a great belch and fell back down onto the blankets.

The Farmer was across the threshold in an instant, with Tibbie chasing at his heels.

When they made it to the cradle, there was their son, cooing and chirruping through his dreams.

'There's only one road left now,' said Old Wullie. 'And it is not a kind one.'

Out by the peat stack, the Farmer and the Tailor talked late into the night about how the worth of a child might be weighed up and measured out in fleeces and skins.

At dawn, Tibbie watched as the men clambered up onto the roof of the cottage and fitted the cuts of turf to the chimney, pinning it down tight, like the stitching of a coat across the broad shoulders of a gentleman.

Then Old Wullie gave his final instruction.

'Whatever you see or hear, come running when the dancing begins,' he said. 'And not one moment after.'

Tibbie and the Farmer watched from behind the strong door, and they waited.

Old Wullie pulled a set of pipes from his pack, set the bellows bag beneath his arm and began to play. It was a hurling, howling sound without grace or melody.

Up out of the cradle came Johnnie-He-Not, his hands clamped over his ears. He grabbed the pipes from Old Wullie's hand and made as if to tear them apart with his teeth.

'Think on,' said Old Wullie. 'That's my bread and butter, my whisky and water. If I've not got my playing, I've got nothing.'

Johnnie-He-Not spat out the leather belly and offered up the instrument.

'Trouble is,' said Old Wullie, 'I'm all out of melodies. I've shared with you in good faith. How's about you share a tune with me?'

Johnnie-He-Not cocked his head. Then he stuffed the belly-bag beneath his arm, wrapped his twig-twisted fingers around the chanter, stuck the blowpipe into the gash-grimace of his mouth and began to play. It was a rollicking reel, whipping wild through the air.

In the cold outside, Tibbie was caught by a breath of memory. The threshing barn crammed to bursting, the fiddle, the whistle and the drum. Her wedding gown hitched up around her waist as the Farmer's son, the boy all the village girls were after and the one she got, hauled her up in his arms and set her spinning.

Old Wullie stood suddenly, striking up a jig, his hobnail boots sparking on the flagstones.

'More!' cried the Tailor. 'And stronger!'

Johnnie-He-Not let out a great yelp, leapt down from the cradle and caught Old Wullie's outstretched arm, whirling widdershins, faster and faster.

Tibbie and the Farmer came quick through the door and braced their backs against it.

Johnnie-He-Not dropped the pipes and made to bolt for the cradle. But Old Wullie had a tight hold on him. He swung out, back and up, and sent the creature flying straight into the fire.

A stew of smoke filled the room to blindness. The screeching and scrabbling shook the chimney stack. Tibbie held on to her husband and they stood firm together.

Then there was silence.

Beyond the silence there came a sound, from directly outside, like the mewling of a kitten. Tibbie crouched down at the keyhole and saw, on the doorstep, as naked and as perfect as the day he was born, her True Johnnie.

She held her bonny boy tight and watched on as the men went up onto the roof and un-stoppered the chimney. The turf crumbled in their hands and if they found anything else caught amongst it, they spoke of that to no one.

From that day on, Tibbie and her husband faced the trials of life together, standing side by side in all matters. Tibbie counted her blessings daily. Under the Tailor's quiet instruction, she set a pair of pins crosswise beneath her son's pillow every night. On her husband's insistence, they always slept with a stout poker at the bedside.

As for Old Wullie, he left the farm that night whistling, full of plans of how he might stitch together his new-found fortunes. The next morning, his pack was discovered by the side of the road, stuffed to bursting with lambswool and strong tanned leather. But the good Tailor was never seen again.

THE BLACK BULL'S BRIDE

Once there was a widowed Washerwoman who had three daughters. As they grew more beautiful and more bold with each passing year, she knew full well that they would not be content to be kept by her forever.

So it was, one fine Spring morning her Eldest Daughter came skipping down the stairs.

'Bake me a bannock, Mother,' she said. 'For I'm ready to set out to meet my Fate.'

The Washerwoman went to work. But she was not as nimble with the folding of the dough as she was with the squaring up of linen. When she pulled the bannock from the stove it was sump-middled with one good golden side and the other burnt to black. The Washerwoman cut it up and turned to her daughter.

'Which will it be?' she said. 'The good half for present pleasure, or the bad half with my life-long blessing?'

The Eldest Daughter did not meet her mother's eye as she slipped the good half into her apron pocket and closed the kitchen door behind her.

She sat on the back steps of the cottage, looking out at the lane ahead. Day turned to a night speckled with stars and she wished on each and every one.

The following day and night passed in the same fashion.

Then at dawn, over the brow of the hill came a golden carriage with six black steeds set before it, their jewelled bridles jumping and jangling.

'Well then,' said the Washerwoman, 'that's for you.'

As Spring turned to Summer, the Middle Daughter was often found out in the yard, stretching a minute's work to an hour as she pinned the sheets to the line always with one eye on the far horizon.

It was Midsummer when she came skipping down the stairs with her Elder Sister's words upon her tongue.

'Bake me a bannock, Mother,' she said. 'For I'm ready to set out to meet my Fate.'

The Washerwoman set her skills to the stove with the best of intentions, but once more the bannock was burnt and blighted. Once more she cut bad from good and offered up the choice.

The Middle Sister took the unspoilt half without a word of thanks or farewell.

For two days and two nights she sat upon the step staring out at the long lane, with only her dreams and desires for company.

At dawn on the third day, over the brow of the hill there came a silver carriage drawn by four white steeds with glass bells set upon their silver bridles, chattering and chiming.

'Well then,' said the Washerwoman, 'that's for you.'

From that day on, the Youngest Daughter took on all the tasks that her sisters had so easily abandoned, and she did so without complaint.

One brisk Autumn morning, the Washerwoman arose at dawn to find her Youngest Daughter already setting the iron to the linen. She saw the frown etched upon that fair face and the slight stoop of her bonny back.

The Washerwoman raked up the coals and took her mixing bowl from the shelf.

When she pulled the burnt bannock from the stove her Youngest Daughter would not touch it. She declared that she would sooner have a man of the fields than she would let herself be taken away in a shining carriage steered by an unseen stranger.

The Washerwoman shook her head. She had raised her three girls as equal and that is how they would be favoured.

When all her arguments were exhausted, the Youngest Daughter cut the black crusts from the bannock and left the warmth of hearth and home for the darkness of the doorstep. There she sat and wept for two days and two nights, but the door at her back remained locked against her.

Dawn of the third day brought with it a foggy dew that came in close and thick. The world beyond the doorstep was a white stew of nothing. Then there came a sound, like the beating of a drum, shaking the earth and the air.

The mist was torn apart by a pair of pointed horns and a great snout set with a golden ring. A Black Bull was stood before her, hair-backed, wild-eyed and stamping.

The Washerwoman was at the door, offering up her own heart, her life, her soul for all eternity if the beast might accept her as his companion in the place of her Youngest and Dearest Daughter.

The Black Bull roared out a refusal.

'Fate is Fate, Mother,' said the Youngest Daughter. 'And this one's for me.' She climbed upon the back of the Black Bull, and they rode off together.

The world beyond the village boundary was as strange as it was beautiful. There were lush green mountains and great lakes that mirrored them, doubling the wonders of this wild land as they rode through it.

The Youngest Daughter broke the burnt bannock. With each mouthful she took, she fed an equal share to the Black Bull. He licked her fingers with his rasping tongue and they went on.

Soon all was eaten, but still the road unfolded before them, upwards and onwards. The Youngest Daughter felt hunger churning deep in her belly, and she pressed her face into the nape of the Black Bull's neck.

'Share and share alike,' said he. 'There's meat in my right ear and drink in my left. Sup softly and take your fill.'

The meat was tender, the drink was sweet, and as the Youngest Daughter ate and drank and shared all out evenly, a contentment came over her. Sleep swiftly followed it.

In her dream, she saw a shingled beach by a vast sea and a black sky above it. There was a man carrying her in his arms, down to the waters. He was dark-haired, broad-shouldered and his eyes were kind. There was a slender ship with a curved prow, like a wave worked from wood. He laid her down upon a blanket of fur in the belly of the boat and unfurled a strong, squared sail. The ship went racing across the ocean, with the wild waves turning and tumbling beneath.

It was the turning and tumbling that woke her – the heaving of the flanks of the Black Bull as he thundered on. Their road was now winding through different mountains – grey, cruel-cragged, snow-crested and lifeless.

'Fear not,' said the Black Bull. 'This is the land of my Eldest Brother. He will shelter us.'

No sooner had the words been spoken than there ahead was a grand castle enclosed by a strong sandstone wall with an iron-anchored gate. They rode into the courtyard where a white-haired man with all the cares and laughter of his life etched upon his face stood waiting.

The King of the Mountains and his Queen welcomed in the travellers, and they feasted together in the great hall. But as the sun began to slip behind the tallest peak, the Black Bull bowed his horned head and took his leave.

The Queen of the Mountains led the Youngest Daughter to a grand chamber. There was a soft bed and a fire blazing in the hearth, but she could not settle.

She crept down to the stables. There were the King's fine horses, with their grooms sleeping upon the straw beside them. She came to a strong wooden door, fastened with an iron chain. She set her cheek against the wood and softly sang.

'Down the long roads you came for me,
Across high lands you carried me,
Your meat and drink you shared with me,
My wild strange husband, I shall not desert thee.'

And there upon the cold floor she lay down and she slept.

She woke to find herself in her bedchamber. From the edges of her sleep, there came the whisper of a dream. Strong arms lifting her up from the floor, a blanket set about her shoulders.

Looking out from her window, she saw in the courtyard below the Black Bull was pacing, setting the cobbles ringing. She made to go to him, but the Queen of the Mountains took her aside and pulled a ripe red apple from her pocket.

'Take this,' she said. 'There shall come a time when you find yourself in great peril and you shall feel your heart breaking. Then and only then, split this fruit apart.'

The Youngest Daughter did not question the instruction. Instead, she thanked the Queen kindly, climbed upon the Black Bull's back and they rode on.

Down the steep slope they thundered, until they came to a lake, stretching before and beneath, dark and deep. 'Fear not,' said the Black Bull. 'This is the land of my Middle Brother. He will shelter us.'

No sooner had the words been spoken than there ahead was a grand castle, with a double ring of limestone walls, both with a brass-barbed gate. In the courtyard beyond, a handsome man in the prime of his years stood waiting.

The King and Queen of the Lake welcomed in the travellers and laid out a fine banquet. But as the water ran red-gold, mirroring the turning sky, the Black Bull took his leave once more.

Once more the Youngest Daughter deserted her bedchamber in favour of sheets of straw, pillowing her cheek against a brass-bolted door as she sang her lullaby.

'Down the long roads you came for me,
Across high lands you carried me,
Your meat and drink you shared with me,
My wild strange husband, I shall not desert thee.'

Again, she woke to find herself returned to the bedchamber. As she shook herself free of sleep, something lingered – the touch of a kiss upon her forehead.

Looking out from her window she saw the Black Bull pawing up the clay of the lakeside below, hooves, horns and snout doubled as he bent his broad back and drank.

She made to go to him, but the Queen of the Lake took her aside and pulled a gleaming green pear from her pocket.

'Take this,' she said. 'There shall come a time when you find yourself in danger that is greater than the greatest you have known, and you shall feel your heart breaking and breaking again. Then and only then, split this fruit apart.'

The Youngest Daughter did not question the instruction. Instead, she thanked the Queen kindly and climbed upon the Black Bull's back.

No sooner had she done so than he gave out a great roar and leapt into the lake. His hooves churned the dark water into spitting spume, where creatures without faces or fins writhed and wrestled.

On and through they thundered. When the depths turned to shallows, the Youngest Daughter saw a vast forest ahead, the trees ranked up like sentinels of the shoreline.

'Fear not,' said the Black Bull. 'This is the land of my Youngest Brother. He will shelter us.'

No sooner had the words been spoken than there ahead was a grand quartz castle, encircled by three walls, each with a silver-spiked gate. In the courtyard at the heart of the fortress there stood a fair-haired boy King, his features untroubled by the weathering of time.

The King of the Forest and his child-Queen welcomed in the travellers. There was rich food and strong wine but on this third night the Youngest Daughter ate little and drank less. She watched as the setting sun fell slow and sure until it was caught by the branches of the tallest tree. When the Black Bull took his leave she followed swiftly, running through the twisted cloisters of that thrice-walled castle until she came to the stables.

From the other side of the silver-shackled door came a savage screaming – part beast, part man.

The Youngest Daughter stood firm and cried out her song.

'Down the long roads you came for me,
Across high lands you carried me,
Your meat and drink you shared with me,
My wild strange husband, I shall not desert thee.'

There was a sudden silence, as if the world and everything in it was holding its breath.

Then the chains unravelled and the door opened.

Stood before her was a man. He was dark-haired, broad-shouldered, his eyes were kind, and he had a black blanket of fur cast around his shoulders. The moment she looked upon him she knew him. Her dreams were not dreams at all, but the truth of her husband's nature.

As they lay together on that bullhide blanket he told her his tale. Before he became beast he was known as the King of the Land of Plenty. He told of the web of enchantment that held him and of how her kindness and courage had loosened the knots of it. Now he might inhabit his true form, by night or by day. Whichever side of sunset she favoured was hers for the taking.

She saw how it could be. A castle and a kingdom of their own ruling. Wealth and worship, feasting and flattery until sundown. Followed by cold nights, without comfort or company.

Or it could be the opposite.

As dawn broke the Black Bull's Bride placed the hide across her husband's back and held on tight fast through the horrors and the howling as his bones shifted. When she returned to her bedchamber she watched from the window as he paced the edge of the wild wood, slicing at the bramble and bracken with his horns, cutting out the path they would take together.

She made to go to him, but the Queen of the Forest was suddenly at her side, pulling a plump purple plum from her pocket.

'Take this,' she said. 'There shall come a time when you find yourself in the greatest danger that the world could hold for you, and you shall feel your heart set to break three times over. Then and only then, split this fruit apart.'

The Black Bull's Bride smiled to hear the instruction. It was as she had told her own dear mother. Rather an honest match than a man who comes courting with gold and silver but keeps his true nature unseen and unknown. Her husband's enchantment held neither danger nor heartbreak for her.

Nonetheless, she thanked the Queen kindly and climbed upon the Black Bull's back and they rode out into the thick of the forest together.

The world turned towards year's end. The beasted days ran short and the nights were love-long. Where they rode and where they rested, I do not know. But on Midwinter's Day they came to a grey glen. At the centre of it stood a stump of slate. The Black Bull lowered his bride down upon it.

'Here I must leave you, my love,' he said. 'For I must go to fight the Old One and settle our affairs for all time.'

He told her the part she must play in the matter. How she must sit stock still upon that stack of stone and wait for revelation.

If the land around her turned red, then the Old One will have claimed mastery over him and he would be bull-bound for the rest of his years. But if all turned rich Royal blue, the Old One will have been vanquished and all their hardships would be behind them.

Whichever way the scales of battle fell, he vowed she would be given free choice of her own Fate: to be his dearest for all her days, or to not. But one thing was certain: if she moved an inch before he returned, they would be forever lost to one another.

The Black Bull's Bride went to her apron and offered up her articles of protection: apple, pear and plum from mountain, lake and forest.

'This is not your trouble nor yet is it your time,' said the Black Bull. And with that, he was gone.

The day turned to night and back again as the Black Bull's Bride waited for the world to change.

It began at the bracken. It ran red from the root upwards to the very tip, as if sap had been charmed to blood. The Black Bull's Bride felt her heart beating fit to burst from her chest but she sat statue-still and she watched on.

The fern flared fire gold for a moment and then blanched to a steel blue that ran quick up the ivy roping the tree trunks, spreading across bark and branch until the land below and the sky melded into one another, and all was bright and beautiful.

Caught in the wonder of the moment, the Black Bull's Bride clapped her hands in delight. The sound cracked the air and the glen and all within it was gone.

It was as if she had been returned to the start of her own story. She was standing in a thick white mist and she could see no further than the hand that she held out before her.

She took out the ripe red apple.

As she did so, she saw there beneath her feet was a path of spiked, sparkling ice.

Where there's a way there's hope, she thought. And whilst there is hope, the heart holds true. So she tucked that apple back into her pocket and she set out.

She walked until the shoes upon her feet were rent to ribbons. Then she found she could go no further. The air ahead turned suddenly solid. A wall of glass reared up before her, keeping her from whatever lay beyond it. Or keeping something in.

There staring out from the heart of the shining barricade was a tangle-haired, wild-eyed, tatter-clad girl.

The Black Bull's Bride reached out her hand. The stranger echoed her. In that moment she understood, it was not only her husband who had been so savagely transformed by Fate.

The Black Bull's Bride walked the run of the wall. The smooth escarpment gave way to crevice and crag. As her unfamiliar self bent and buckled at her side, she saw that this brutal boundary was not a thing crafted by man. It was a mountain of glass that stretched beyond sight and thought and there was no way round, over or through.

As she went to her apron, her shadow-self also plucked a gleaming green pear from the pocket.

There, over the shoulder of the girl she had become, she saw a flickering light. A fire. Then a sound came echoing down the air, like the beating of a division bell – iron upon iron.

The Black Bull's Bride ran as fast as bloodied feet on ice shingle could carry her to the threshold of that forge.

The Blacksmith set down his tools and listened as she told the tale of her beastly-bodied, noble-hearted husband. She told of his instruction and her betrayal of it and of how all she loved was now lost to her for eternity.

'Eternity is evermore in some worlds,' said the Blacksmith. 'And in others it is not.'

He stirred the coals, and the flames leapt.

'In the place where ice and fire meet nothing is forever fixed.'

The Blacksmith set out his bargain. He would give shelter

and lodging in return for an apprenticeship served. Then they would see what they might see at the end of it.

Where there's work there is a way, she thought. And where there's a way there's hope. And whilst there is hope, the heart holds true.

So she tucked that pear back into her pocket and stepped across the threshold.

For seven long years she worked without complaint. She turned washerwomen's tasks – hauling water, fetching fuel, sweeping and scrubbing – to a man's purpose.

She set herself to the bellows and learned the art of breath-building that tempered flame.

She learned the piecework, mastering the mechanisms of bolts and brackets that fitted the strong doors of kitchen and stable.

She learned the loosening and the fitting of every shape and size of shackle. From the fence links as fat as her fist to the fingertip filigree of bridle bits. As she wove chain to rein she thought of her two sisters and their unseen suitors and prayed that their roads from cottage door to marriage bed had been kind.

She learned the drawing out and the twisting of weapons. She hammered out spear, shield and the nine-folded sword and cast them into the blanching basin. As the white-hot metal cooled to blue steel the Black Bull's Bride saw ivy, bark and blossom shining bright in victory.

Then as the seventh year rolled round, she set to the making of her own metal.

She fashioned iron sole, heel, toe and tongue and married them together into her apprentice-piece.

The air chimed anew as iron shoes met glass mountain. The Black Bull's Bride followed her soot-smeared self across the escarpment, upwards and onwards. She wept for love and for the loss of it. Her tears turned to falling ice that skittered beneath her feet, unsteadying her at every step.

She took out the plump purple plum.

As she did so the mist rolled back behind her. She found herself at the clear crest of the crag-top and the land that unfolded before her was the opposite of where she had come from.

A patchwork of fields and farmsteads unfurled beneath. There, at the edge of the land, was a castle hewn from rich red rock, shining like a burning beacon.

Where there's wealth there is work, she thought. And where there's work there's a way. Where there's a way there is hope. And whilst there is hope, the heart holds true.

So she tucked that plum back into her pocket and went on.

At the foot of the mountain was a babbling brook. There she freed herself from her iron shoes, shed her gown and with her mother's skills still in her hands, she wrung out her work-worn dress and scrubbed until it came up clean. She laid it out upon the riverbank, hid her apron beneath and waded out into the water.

How long it took to wash away the muck that seven years of forge and fire sets upon the skin, I do not know. But when the Black Bull's Bride returned to the riverbank, she had company.

There was a girl sat upon the grass.

'Who are you to bathe so boldly in the Royal river?' she said, looking the Black Bull's Bride up and down, with no care for her modesty.

Her face was beautiful but her eyes were cruel.

'I beg pardon and I mean no harm,' said the Black Bull's Bride. 'I am but a tattered traveller, no one of any consequence.'

'Princess or pauper,' said Cruel Eyes, 'a price must be paid for such trespass.'

This was danger indeed and the Black Bull's Bride cursed her foolishness for abandoning her treasures so lightly.

'So best set to work and make good,' said Cruel Eyes, 'or the worse it will go for you.'

She pulled out a red shirt from behind her back and flung it into the water.

The moment the Black Bull's Bride set her hand to the task, the river ran blood-red in an instant and the cloth came up clean. The white silken shirt was set with fine stitches and pearl buttons which winked in the sunlight.

Cruel Eyes snatched the garment from her hand and walked swiftly away. The Black Bull's Bride dried and dressed and ran after.

She came to a cottage at the edge of the forest. She crouched upon the step and set her eye to the keyhole.

There was an Old Mother showering kisses and praise upon her cruel-eyed daughter. The more the Black Bull's Bride heard, the more she understood.

The Black Bull's Bride knocked upon the door and curtseyed deeply when it was answered.

'Pray show grace and favour, My Lady,' she said. 'I am nothing and I have nothing. It would be the greatest honour to be the servant of the linen and laundry of the Queen.'

Cruel Eyes looked her up and down once more, and gave a sharp nod.

The Black Bull's Bride bowed her head and kissed the hand that was held out to her.

The Old Mother watched on silent. In her eyes there was a look that the Black Bull's Bride had seen before – the sadness that comes when the unspoilt half and the easy road has been taken, with no thought of the cost of it.

The Black Bull's Bride walked three paces behind Cruel Eyes and kept her gaze directly upon the path before them, as it twisted and turned and until it came to a golden gate set beneath ramparts of red rock.

Cruel Eyes held up the shirt in a semaphore of surrender and the gate opened.

It went the same way with the three gates in the three walls that followed.

In the courtyard beyond a man with broad shoulders, dark hair and eyes shining with love and tears stood waiting.

The Black Bull's Bride watched as her husband knelt and offered up a golden ring to Cruel Eyes.

The four walls of the castle rang with the fanfare of trumpets and proclamation.

The King of the Land of Plenty had found his True Queen. There would be three days and three nights of feasting and then they would be wed.

The Black Bull's Bride felt the cracking deep inside her. The swift shattering of heartbreak.

She walked three paces behind her beloved as he led his False Bride to her chambers. She watched on as kisses and promises were exchanged and her husband did not once turn to look at her.

The instant after he departed, the Black Bull's Bride took out the ripe red apple and split it apart. There, at the heart of the flesh of the fruit, were pips of ruby.

Cruel Eyes made to snatch the jewels from her hand, but they stuck fast to the palm of the Black Bull's Bride.
    'Such riches must be traded for a gift of equal worth that is freely given,' she said. 'Let me lie for one night in the Royal bedchamber and they shall be yours.'
    Cruel Eyes gave consent without question or thought.

But thought came creeping in as twilight fell.
    Cruel Eyes recalled the stories that had travelled the length and breadth of the land. How the King had vanished at the hunt on All Hallow's Eve, only to be found on Midwinter's Day roaming the forest, mad and weeping. All that he had was the bloodied rags upon his back and the prophecy that he spoke. Of how his shirt could only be washed clean by a girl of true pure heart. She and she alone would have the power to return him to himself.

She thought of how the King's guardsmen had summoned the daughters of noblemen, merchants and even the farmers before they had deigned to come knocking at her Old Mother's door.

She thought of how in the world of men, cunning was a quality to be celebrated. Why should it not go the same way for her?

Cruel Eyes went to the Royal kitchen. There she mixed herbs and spices, milk and honey and other elements besides. She sent it up to the Royal bedchamber as a token of her affection.

At the chiming of the midnight bell, the Black Bull's Bride moved as silent as shadow, slipping past the sleeping guards, and turned the key of her husband's door.

She went to the bed, pulled back the curtains and lay beside him. She set her cheek upon the goose-down pillow and wept as she sang.

'Seven long years I served for thee.
The glassy hill I climbed for thee.
Thy bloody shirt I wrang for thee.
And wilt thou not waken and turn to me?'

Still he slept on.

As the cock crowed in the new day, the Black Bull's Bride felt the faultline of her heart crack deeper and darker as she went creeping back to the chamber of her cruel mistress.

She took out the gleaming green pear and split it. There, cast starwise in the centre, were pips of emeralds.

That morning the King came down to the banquet hall whistling. He declared how his beloved bride was worthy of the finest wedding feast. So he would set out with the best and boldest hunter in the land – the King of the Forest.

The two brothers rode out side by side. But the King of the Forest's brow was frown-furrowed with care. His spear flew wide and reckless, time and time again missing the mark.

'What ails you, Youngest Brother,' said the King, 'that you should be so at odds with your own nature?'

The King of the Forest fretted at the hilt of his sword and when he spoke the words came in a whisper.

'Brother dearest,' he said. 'Such weeping and wailing there was coming from your chamber last night. Such night terrors cry out a warning. I fear the Fate that lies ahead for you.'

The King of the Land of Plenty laughed away his brother's words. He assured him he had been untroubled by dreams of any kind. It was the folly of youth to mistake the run of the winds about the four strong walls for the cries of a condemned man.

Meanwhile, back in the castle, the Black Bull's Bride offered up the emeralds. Cruel Eyes had but to look upon them and her blood ran green with envy. She mixed her sleeping draught with cunning and caution – and she doubled the dosage accordingly.

The second night went the same way as the first.

The Black Bull's Bride lay with her husband's back braced against her as she wept and sang.

'Seven long years I served for thee.
The glassy hill I climbed for thee.
Thy bloody shirt I wrang for thee.
And wilt thou not waken and turn to me?'

The dawn broke, and with it her heart also shattered – like a looking glass that once held a true image, fractured into a cobweb of confusion.

Back in her cruel mistress's chamber, the Black Bull's Bride took out the plump purple plum and split it apart. The stone at the heart of the flesh was an amethyst, hewn diadem perfect.

That morning the King once more declared he would fashion a feast worthy of his bride, what matter whether fish or flesh? He would take to the riverside with his Middle Brother, for there was no other in the land who could match his skill with the hook and the net.

The Black Bull's Bride sat quietly beside her simpering mistress and thought of how she might contest the truth of this, but she held her peace.

The two brothers sat side by side at the babbling brook. The salmon leapt joyfully upstream, as if offering themselves willingly to the Royal banquet. But the King of the Lake fixed bait to barb with trembling fingers and every line he cast roved wildly.

'What ails you, Middle Brother,' said the King, 'that you should be so at odds with your own nature?'

The King of the Lake fretted at the tip of his hook and when he spoke the words came in a whisper.

'Brother dearest,' he said. 'Such weeping and wailing there was coming from your chamber last night. It was a voice not your own. Such a ghostly visitation carries a warning. I fear the Fate that lies ahead for you.'

The King of the Land of Plenty laughed away his brother's words. He assured him he had been untroubled by any kind of apparition. If he was to believe the tales of Henwives and Simpletons, he would not be able to walk the length of his grand hall without passing through a hundred unseen spirits. It was the folly of middle age to set superstition against common sense.

Back in the castle, the Black Bull's Bride offered up the amethyst. Cruel Eyes agreed to the bargain before it was brokered.

Then it was not cunning or caution that Cruel Eyes stirred into her sleeping draught that night.

It was triumph.

At dawn she would send the guardsmen to her husband's chamber and there would be sharp justice indeed for the maid who had betrayed her mistress and thought to turn the King against his prophecy-proved purpose.

This would be a stain that could not be wrung clean. The secrets that this washerwoman held against her would be forever silenced, at the end of a dropped rope.

That night, at the Wedding Eve Feast, the King noticed how his Eldest Brother did not share the merriment of the hall. Rather he sat frowning at his plate, and when the feasting gave way to the dancing, he swiftly left the table.

The King followed, and found him standing in the open courtyard, face turned to the sky.

'What ails you, Eldest Brother,' said the King, 'that you would set yourself apart from celebration and good company, in a manner so at odds with your own nature?'

'It is but the torment of time,' said the King of the Mountains. 'I will soon be at the limit of my years. My mind is as restless as my bones are weary.'

He gestured up to scattered stars above.

'I do confess, I fear the Fate that lies ahead for me, in the unknown world beyond.'

The King of the Land of Plenty slung his arm around his brother's stooped shoulders and spoke softly.

He told of the tricks his own broken mind had played upon him from the day that he was found wandering the forest with his name and nature lost to him. Dreadful dreams of a grey glen, a mountain made of glass, a blistering fire – and running through all of it, the thundering beat of a drum.

Then he told of the sweet sleeping draught made by the hand of his Pure-Hearted Bride and how it had brought an end to his torment.

'I will instruct her to attend to you in the same fashion,' he said. 'And you will rest easy.'

The King of the Mountains shook his head and smiled. 'Dearest brother, I fear a part of you is still caught in your own unknowing. Never forget the greatest duty of True Kingship. We must face our fears with full knowledge, not turn our backs upon them.'

When the King of the Land of Plenty retired to his bedchamber that night, he poured the sleeping draught down into the gaps between the floorboards. The rats soon ceased their scratching.

He set his cheek to the pillow, his face to the wall and kept his senses sharpened.

There came the midnight bell and with it the turning of the key in the lock, the cold rush of air as the curtains of his bed were parted. There was a shifting of the sheets and the warmth of a body pressed against his back and a sweet voice singing.

'Seven long years I served for thee.
The glassy hill I climbed for thee.
Thy bloody shirt I wrang for thee.
And wilt thou not waken and turn to me?'

He turned and looked into the eyes of the woman in the bed beside him. He remembered whom and what he had once been and all that had passed between them.

When Cruel Eyes rose at the first light of dawn, she found the guardsmen she meant to summon already outside her bedchamber with their swords drawn.

When the King of the Land of Plenty led his Bride into the grand hall the last knots of enchantment loosened. All who looked upon her saw her True nature. All that was lost was now found.

Cruel Eyes was brought before them. She knelt at the feet of the Royal thrones and pleaded for pardon.

'A mortal man may show mercy,' said the King. 'But I speak with the authority of the Black Bull that thunders. As you would do to others, so shall it be done to you.'

The False Bride was bound hand and foot. Some folk say that her strong shackles were forged by the True Queen herself.

In the depths of the dungeon Cruel Eyes was given a bed of straw and cinders. She was offered a crust of burnt bread soaked in milk and honey and bitter herbs of forgetting.

Whether she chose to lose her knowledge of herself or if she spent the remains of her allotted life in full understanding of her Fate, I do not know.

The Bull King of the Land of Plenty wed his Girl of True Pure Heart. She wore a handsome wedding crown, bedecked with rubies for love, emeralds for peace and the proud shining amethyst for the healing of heart and mind. There in the red castle, behind the four walls and the four locks of the golden gates, they lived happily ever after.

STEALING THE MOON

Jack was down on his luck. He had not a penny to his name. His boots were battered to breaking, his coat was worn thread-thin. His pack was empty – he had no tools with which to ply an honest trade and all that he had to defend himself from the thieves and vagabonds of the long roads was a blunt butterknife poking through a hole in his back pocket.

As he walked the lanes of the village that fresh Spring night, the full moon was shining above like a great silver coin and Jack felt that even the sky itself was mocking his plight. But the more he thought upon this, the more his wits sharpened.

He came to the village green, with the wide-walled well set at the heart of it. Then there was the inn, with laughter and singing drifting out of the open window on the warm breeze. Jack pushed open the door and walked across the threshold. The room fell silent and the faces that turned to him were faces of men he knew.

There was the fat Farmer, with his sun-scorched skin. Slung across his back was a cattle rope and he had his boots propped up against the hearth. Beside him sat the broad-backed Woodcutter, with his keen-bladed axe leaning against his chair. Beside him was the Soldier, standing straight and stern, in his jacket bedecked with medals and with his sword hanging handsomely at his side. Leaning across the bar, haggling pennies for the price of a bottle of brandy, was the Merchant in his fine long coat, fitted with too many pockets to count, all fixed with gleaming gold buttons. Beside him stood the broad-bellied Bishop of the Lands who had folded his sermons of sobriety back inside his Bible for the evening and was filling his goblet up to the brim with wine that was as red and rich as the ruby set in the golden band of his Holy Ring.

'We want none of your trouble tonight, Jack,' said the Innkeeper. 'Full and fair payment before you set a foot further.'

'It's not trouble I'm bringing,' replied Jack. 'But opportunity.'

Then he turned to the assembled company and asked them if they had ever given any thought to how the stars were placed in the sky and what caused them to shine so bright?

'How else but by the hand and the will of the Almighty Himself?' declared the Bishop.

'Without question, Your Worship,' said Jack. 'But do you have knowledge of the exact material that Our Good Lord, in his great wisdom, chose to forge the stars from?'

The Bishop muttered into his goblet some words about the infinite mysteries of the Heavens.

'As Old Mistress Henwife told it to me,' said Jack, 'I now tell it to you. The moon is made of silver and when it turns from full to thin, that is the hand of God breaking pieces from it slice by slice and scattering them across the firmament for our delight.'

As Jack spoke, the Farmer thought of all the skies that he had laboured under through every season and every hour. He brushed the mud from his boots.

'There's sense in that,' he said. 'I've seen with my own eyes how the stars shine brighter when the moon's on the wane.'

Then Jack told of the great wonder he had witnessed. How that very night he'd seen the fat full moon slip from its fixing and come crashing down into the village well. He told how if he could only find one strong man, brave and true, who would be willing to help him, they could haul the fortune of the fallen moon out together. Then they could take it to the Blacksmith to break on his anvil. Then they would share their winnings out even and they'd both walk away with pockets full of silver.

Before another man could say a word in either favour or protest, the Farmer was up from his seat with his cattle rope in hand, heading out of the door with Jack running after.

They came to the well and the Farmer was wrapping the rope around his waist and holding the other end out to Jack. Just as the Farmer was about to pitch himself over the edge, Jack turned and whispered in his ear.

'Those are fine and heavy boots you have,' Jack said. 'A strength on the land, but a weakness in the water. Take care, my friend. Wealth in the pockets of a drowned man is no wealth at all.'

Greed is a blindness. The Farmer unlaced his boots and set them aside. Down into the well the Farmer went, slipping and cursing.

Jack held the end of the rope tight in his fist and he waited.

'There's a fortune here sure enough,' called the Farmer. 'But the moon is stuck and I haven't the strength to lift it.'

'Sit tight,' said Jack. 'I know just the man we need.'

He tied the end of the rope to a nearby tree stump and he went running back to the inn with the Farmer's demand.

As Jack spoke, the Woodcutter thought of all the timber he had cut and fashioned, from the hazel poles of the Shepherd Boy's crook to the broad oak beams of the great hall of the Lord of the Land.

'There's sense in that,' he said. 'A fat full moon will sit heavier on the shoulders than a sickly slice of silver. It wants splitting.'

Before another man could say a word in either favour or protest, the Woodcutter was up from his seat, placing his axe in his belt and striding out of the door with Jack.

They came to the well, with the Farmer bellowing up at them from the belly of it.

Jack untied the rope from the stump and just as the Woodcutter was setting it around himself, Jack turned and whispered in his ear.

'That's a smartly sharpened axe you have,' Jack said. 'Why risk the rusting of it? I'll warrant that a man with your strength can break apart a sheet of silver with fists and feet alone.'

Pride is a blindness. The Woodcutter unhooked the shining axe from his belt and set it aside. Down into the well the Woodcutter went, as swiftly as a stone dropped from the hand of a child to test the depth of it.

The splashing and cursing doubled.

Jack held the end of the rope tight in his fist and he waited.

'There's a fortune here sure enough,' called the Woodcutter. 'That moon broke easy. But now there's nothing but argument about how to carry it up.'

'Sit tight,' said Jack. 'I know just the man we need.'

He tied the rope to the stump once more and he went running back to the inn with the Woodcutter's complaint.

As Jack spoke, the Soldier played with the golden medals on his chest. He thought of all the honours that he had won in every corner of the Kingdom – and how none of them were for kindness.

'There's sense in that,' he said. 'It takes a certain strength of character to command the uncouth and the unruly.'

Before another man could say a word in either favour or protest, the Soldier stepped forward. He had one hand on the hilt of his sword and the other on Jack's elbow as he marched him out of the inn.

They came to the well and the tree stump beside it. The Soldier sliced through the knot with a single swipe of the sword and Jack caught the quick run of the rope as it was released. The Soldier grabbed it from his hand and he was setting it about Jack's own waist when Jack turned and whispered in his ear.

'It is an honour to be under your command, Sir,' Jack said. 'No man standing before you could doubt your authority. But consider the deception of the echo cast by well-stone and water. I fear that if you issue orders from above then your voice will assume a weakness that it does not possess.'

Vanity is a blindness. The Soldier praised Jack for his astute assessment of the terrain and accordingly considered him a man worthy to be entrusted with the safekeeping of his sword as he set it aside and bound himself with twice-twisted knots. Down into the well the Soldier went with slow, steady steps of stealth and intention.

Jack held the end of the rope tight in his fist and he waited.

'There's a fortune here sure enough,' called the Soldier. 'We are swimming in a thousand pieces of silver. However, these insubordinates refuse to take instruction on how to share it out according to our individual worth and station.'

'Sit tight,' said Jack. 'I know just the man we need.'

He tied the rope to the tree stump once more, a little tauter and tighter after the massacre of the knot. Then he went running back to the inn with the Soldier's dilemma.

As Jack spoke, the Merchant patted down his own pockets. He thought of all the names in all the ledger books that were stacked up on his shelves, and all the percentages set in their margins.

Before the Bishop could say a word in either favour or protest, the Merchant stepped up to Jack and pulled out his pocketbook and pen.

'There's sense in that,' he said. 'The ignorant man has a tendency to overestimate his own worth and indeed the payment that is his due. I would be willing to consult in this matter for a higher dividend of the profits of the moon.'

Jack had been on the long roads and back again enough times by now to know full well that the moment a man starts using three long words when a short one will do, there's trickery in it. But that night Jack agreed upon the Merchant's terms and conditions and held the door open for him as he strutted out of the inn.

When they reached the edge of the well, the Merchant grew pale and he began to tremble.

'I would take your instructions down there myself, Sir,' said Jack. 'And I would do it gladly. But which man amongst them would accept any assessment of acumen from a ragged ruffian like myself?'

The Merchant nodded and held his arms out so that Jack might fix the rope to his waist. Then Jack turned and whispered in his ear.

'Consider for a moment the ruinous nature of the water,' Jack said. 'Your book of credit and calculations will spoil in an instant, as will your fine coat.'

Cunning is a blindness. The Merchant fixed all the buttons of all his pockets, folded his long coat up tightly and set it aside. Down into the well the Merchant went, with creeping caution.

Jack held the end of the rope tight in his fist and he waited.

He could only be certain that the Merchant had reached the water when the quarrel echoed up the walls to him. Eventually the men shouted themselves into silence. Then the Merchant called up to Jack.

'There's fortune here sure enough,' he said. 'And the correct division has been agreed upon. However, the silver is slipping between our fingers as we attempt the collection.'

'Sit tight,' said Jack. 'There is but one man left in the world who might help us.'

He tied the short tail end of the rope to the tree stump, straining to hook it. Then he went running back to the inn in search of a miracle.

As Jack spoke, the Bishop turned his gold and ruby ring around his finger. He thought of how his faithful followers knelt before him on his command, in abject awe of the transformation of bread and wine and forever grateful for the subsequent salvation of their souls.

'There's sense in that,' he said. 'If God has deigned to bless us with a Heavenly fortune, then it will take the hand of the Holy Man to claim it.'

Jack bowed his head in supplication and followed in the wake of the Bishop's billowing red robes as he made his processional passage to the well.

The Bishop did not flinch at all as Jack tied the rope around him. Rather, he declared how the Good Lord protects his Chosen One and how this world held not the dangers for him that it might hold for the more common man.

Jack turned and whispered in his ear. 'There is none more worthy of the favour of the Almighty,' he said. 'But ought you not to consider the sacred symbol of your calling? If the Holy Ring slipped from your finger during the course of your perilous descent, then how might your Authority be understood by the unenlightened?'

More than anything else in the known world it is Power – and the possibility that it might be lost – that blinds a man.

The Bishop took his Holy Ring from his finger and set it aside, insisting that Jack swear on his own soul for the surety of its safekeeping.

Down into the well the Bishop went, singing hymns of Holy Water.

He landed with the full force of a cannon ball, the spray soaking Jack to the skin as he peered over the lip of the well, with the last inch of the rope held tight in his fist. He watched the tethered floating congregation paddling around the belly of the Bishop, heads bowed and hands clasped as he bestowed blessings in expectation of riches to come.

'Amen!' called the Bishop as he made the sign of the cross before him.

The Farmer, the Woodcutter, the Soldier and the Merchant all echoed the gesture and so did Jack.

The rope slipped from his fingers and slithered down the wellside like a snake.

Then Jack put on the sturdy boots, placed the axe at one side of his belt and the sword at the other, buttoned the long coat up to the collar, slipped the gold and ruby ring upon his finger and set out. The smiling moon above lit the road ahead as Jack went on his way, whistling.

And there we must leave the Farmer, the Woodcutter, the Soldier, the Merchant and the Bishop, whose folly blinded them to common sense so that they only saw the world that they wanted to see. Whether they ever found a way to set aside greed, pride, vanity, cunning and power in favour of the greater good, I do not know. Perhaps they are down there still, squabbling over a fortune as false as their hearts.

THE TROLL KING'S SISTER

O nce there was an Old King in the North Lands, and
he was dying.

He called his only son Sigurd to him. 'Duty is
sacrifice,' he said. 'It is time to set aside the freedoms of youth
and accept both the honour and demands of your station.'

Sigurd called counsel with the Royal Advisors. They
bowed their heads in sorrow and respect. Then they rolled
out a multitude of arguments and opinions regarding strong
borders and shrewd couplings.

In the days that followed, Sigurd watched on as the daughters
of noblemen were paraded before him and he felt nothing
but despair. For whilst the Old King was ruled by his mind
– by logic and legality – Sigurd was ruled by his heart, by his
dreams and desires.

There was one particular dream that called to Sigurd through
the long nights of his father's illness. A vision of a woman
with fair hair and blue eyes, dressed all in white, standing on
the battlements of a silver castle set at the edge of a wild and
tumbling sea. And although the many daughters of the many
noblemen were beautiful and clever and kind, they were not her.

Sigurd went once more to his father's chamber and told him
the truth of his heart's desire. The Old King smiled to hear it.

The Silver Castle of the Furthest North was a place he knew from the days of his own youth and adventure.

'A King is both ruler and protector,' he said. 'I would gladly depart from this world in the knowledge that my son has secured an alliance that embraces the entirety of the ocean.'

He ordered his longship to be made ready and to be fitted with his finest oarsmen.

Then he called his son to him for the final time.

'Fear not the unfolding of your Fate, my child,' he said. 'It is through the advancement into the unknown that we come to understand our true selves. However long or however hard the journey ahead, all will be well at the end of it.'

So it was that Sigurd set sail across the fierce foaming waters, with a strong wind and his father's blessing behind him.

For a year and a day, Sigurd followed the stars and the sea paths until he came to the shining city of the Furthest North. The King welcomed him into his silver castle. When the King's Youngest Daughter set eyes upon Sigurd, she knew him from her own dreams also. The match was made and they were wed.

The seasons turned and the Princess of the Furthest North gave birth to a strong son. They lived happily and well. Until one morning, there came riding into the courtyard a man dressed all in the black livery of mourning. Sigurd wept to see him, and the Princess wept all the more when she learned of the message that he carried.

The sea that was wild on the setting out rolled easy upon the return. The New Queen took to playing with the young Prince up on the deck, rolling his golden ball across the boards and laughing at his stumbling steps as he ran to catch it.

Then one clear bright morning, a shape appeared on the horizon. A ragged black line, a stain spreading between sea and sky – the high mountain ranges of Sigurd's land. As the Queen gazed upon it, everything changed.

The sea was suddenly becalmed. She looked to the oarsmen. They were slumped in their seats. She looked to her husband at the helm. He too was caught in sleep, fallen at the side of the figurehead. She looked to the ocean once more, and there racing towards her, like a pebble cast across a frozen pond, came a boat.

As it hurtled closer, she saw it for what it truly was: a millstone, with an old woman sat in the hole at the heart of it. The buckle-backed crone tethered her craft to the side of Sigurd's ship. Then with a single leap she was upon the deck. She cackled and she crowed as she plucked the sleeping Prince from his mother's arms.

The scream that rose from the Queen's belly stuck in her throat. She could not move an inch or speak a word as she watched on, frozen.

The Witch placed the boy inside a barrel and sealed him up. She stripped the Queen of her fine robes and exchanged them for her own stinking rags. Then she threw the Queen over the side of the ship, into the centre of the millstone, took the tethering rope between her teeth and bit it free. Thus satisfied, she released the screaming Prince, gathered him up in her crooked embrace and held on tight.

The millstone ground against the waves. The Queen watched as the longship shrunk to a speck and the land came racing towards her. There was a cave at the place where the mountains met the sea. It yawned open and swallowed her up.

Sigurd was woken by a sharp screaming, fit to shake the sky. There was his beautiful Queen, standing at the prow with the Prince beating his tiny fists against her chest. 'It is but the sickness of the sea,' she said sweetly. 'It will pass when we come to land.' King Sigurd looked over his wife's shoulder and he saw the gold glinting turrets of his castle, nestled in the folds of the mountains' peaks. Home.

And yet, he found that his heart was heavy with sorrow. And behind that sorrow, there was a flickering of fear. Then he recalled the wise words of his dear father. He had followed his Fate across the savage seas and returned with his True Queen and a strong son and heir. This position of Kingship was the fitting end to such adventures. This was the correct order of things, and all would be well.

The Prince cried through coronation and feasting and nothing could comfort him. The Royal Advisors frowned into their goblets and muttered behind their sleeves. If a man could not hold sway over his own child, what hope was there for his Kingdom? Once more, Sigurd recalled the wise words of his dear father. Duty is sacrifice. He sent for his old Nursemaid, gave the child unto her care and took up his place in the counting house of the Royal chambers.

There Sigurd set his mind to both the honour and the demands of his station. He knew all too well the nature of the Royal Advisors. They were men of war, men of God and men who were ruled by money. He set his mind to their tricks of rhetoric and as days turned to weeks and then to months, he hardened his heart accordingly in order to set himself in authority over them.

As time passed and the dark Winter drew in, Sigurd saw that it was not only his own heart that had been hardened by the change of lands and circumstance. Since the day that the Prince was taken into the care of the Nursemaid, his dearest Queen had not bestowed one word or one touch of affection on either her son or her husband. Instead, she had ordered a strong door to be built for her bedchamber and bolts set upon the inside of it. Once more, Sigurd recalled the wise words of his dear father. True Kingship is Protection. He ordered his two most trusted guardsmen to sit watch outside his wife's chamber every night.

That is where they were, with a chessboard set between them, when they heard the sound – rumbling rock and scraping stone. They peered through the crack at the hinge of the strong door. The tremor of the floor beneath their feet was matched by the trembling of their very souls as they saw the hearthstone of the Queen's fireplace twisting and turning like the loosening of a lid.

The stone slipped aside and out of the hole beneath came a pair of horns, with a rusted crown balanced between them set upon a great grey head. An iron-toothed, hair-backed, fat-fisted, club-footed creature clambered out into the bedchamber, dragging a tar-tufted tail behind.

The Queen went running into the beast's embrace. Her back buckled, her skin sallowed and her fine features twisted in upon themselves. There she stood: a hook-nosed Witch clad in Royal robes.

'Well met, brother of mine,' she said.

'Well met, sweet sister,' he replied.

He placed his stone-scaled hand upon her head and her skin shifted once more – and out came iron teeth, hagtufted hair and tar-twisted tail.

The troll kin embraced once more, crowing and cackling, the way rocks might laugh if they were given a voice.

The guardsmen crept away from their posts, down to the Royal cellars. They quenched their fears with strong potato wine as they argued their deception into duty.

They were stalwart servants of the King, but were they not also servants of the people? Who would trust the reign of a sovereign who had been tricked into the marriage bed by the Troll King's Sister? Had there not been enough fighting and faction? Let the King remain ignorant of the true nature of his bride, and let the land remain at peace.

The next morning, Sigurd was sat balancing edicts against entreaty when there came a quiet knock on the door of the counting house. There was his Queen, kneeling before him at the threshold whispering her regrets.

She told of how the sudden departure from her beloved homeland had soured her and of how that sourness had turned her own dearest son against her and she was sorry for it. From that day on, she would be the wife and the Queen that was worthy of the Royal household. And most of all, she would be a mother. If the affection of her own flesh and blood had to be slowly earned, then so be it. She would have the Prince sleep in her bedchamber for the three nights following. Then once that time was passed, she would welcome her husband back to her bed.

Sigurd saw that the woman kneeling before him was his True Queen returned – the kind and courtly maiden who had called to him through his dreams. He forgave her trespasses and granted her request with a joyous heart.

He saw then, he had misapprehended the full unfurling of his Fate. There were the adventures that were played out across strange seas and foreign lands. There was also the advancement of understanding gained by an honest examination of heart and mind. Sigurd matched his wife's resolve with his own. His duty as father and husband would not be sacrificed to the cause of Kingship.

The following morning, Sigurd favoured the Queen's chambers over the counting house. They broke the night's fasting together. His wife was all softness and smiles, but his son was not. The Prince sat silent and pale, picking at his plate. When his old Nursemaid came knocking, he ran from the table. She hauled the boy up into her arms and as she did so, Sigurd saw how his son whispered into her ear and he saw the frown upon the Nursemaid's face that followed his words. He turned to his watching wife, her face as blank as stone, and Sigurd felt a cold creeping of Fear.

The second morning went the same as the first. There was his silent son and his sweet wife who turned cold and watchful at the moment of whispering. There was the Nursemaid's furrowed brow. There was that shudder of Fear and the heavy-hearted sorrow close upon the heels of it.

Sigurd returned to his counting house and called the Nursemaid to him. He assured her, whatever his son's secret words might be, there would be no punishment for the speaking of them.

The Nursemaid shook her head.

'It's nothing but the nonsense of a child.'

She chanted it out like a nursery rhyme.

'*One night gone, two days left waking*
Two nights gone, my heart is breaking.'

Suddenly Sigurd felt as if he were adrift upon an open ocean, with no sight of land, his Fate utterly unfixed and uncertain.

That night Sigurd went to the guardsmen and spoke of how any True King would not set a man to a task that he was unwilling to answer to himself. They bowed so deeply that their noses met his boots and departed. Sigurd drew up a chair and sat with the door at his back and the chessboard before him.

By midnight Sigurd had played both sides of himself into stalemate and was contemplating which action was most fitting for a King: to concede a victory or to claim it? Then the black knight hopped from his sentry post and tumbled the white castle.

The floor beneath him was shaking fit to break the flagstones and with it came a terrible shrieking and scraping, as if a great knife was being sharpened upon a giant whetstone.

Sigurd set his shoulder to the door and struck against it until the bolts upon the other side broke from their fixings. He was across the threshold in an instant.

It was as if a mirror had been set down the centre of the room. There was his wife, with their squalling son in her arms. And there, standing directly opposite her, was her double. Except that this second Queen had a thick iron chain set about her waist. A chain that was stretched to straining, rising up from a dark hole where the hearthstone should be.

Sigurd looked from one woman to the next. One clad in the robes of his Kingdom, the other dressed as she had been on their wedding day.

Sigurd's heart yearned towards the bride Queen, but his mind told him strong shackles are always forged for a purpose.

Sigurd took his son from the arms of the unchained Queen and set him down. No sooner than he had done so, the Prince ran laughing to the tethered bride and buried his face in the folds of her skirt.

Sigurd took his sword and struck a savage blow against the iron chain. It broke clean in two, and fell clanking and clattering into the hearthstone hole.

The False Queen let out a scream. Her skin sallowed, her robes ripped to rags as she changed from woman to Witch to Troll. Then she leapt the length of the bedchamber in a single bound and went hurtling down into that hole.

Sigurd held his True Queen close and wept as she told of the enchanted sleep, the millstone boat and the cave that swallowed her. Then she told of how inside that cave there was a river which ran to the gate of the Troll King's castle, hidden in the belly of the mountains.

She told of the dungeon within that castle where the Troll King kept her. She told of his beastly desire and the bargain she had brokered. That if he granted her the freedom to visit her son for three nights, at the end of this allotted time she would become the Troll King's Bride and never again set foot in the World Above. In turn her noble husband would remain bound, unknowing, to the Troll King's Sister. Thus wed, the Tribe of the Trolls would have eternal mastery of the World Above and the World Below.

Then she told of how she had whispered her sorrows into their son's ear and bid him to speak them only to the one whom he loved and trusted above all others. For what greater love is there than that between son and father? And what greater bond of trust than that between Prince and King?

Sigurd called his guardsmen and meted out his judgement. Their table and their chessboard were placed upon the reset hearthstone, and they would play from dusk until dawn upon that very spot, for the rest of their years. Then he called upon his craftsmen to build a second castle, far from the dark shadow of the mountains.

From that day on, King Sigurd vowed that never again would he allow rhetoric and argument to rule over the knowledge of his own heart. He would look upon the world with the honest gaze of a child and he would reign over his Kingdom accordingly, with his True Queen beside him, and all would be well.

The old castle has long since crumbled to ruins, and the winding roads through the mountains swallowed by rockfall.

But the land remains restless. The earth twists as if trying to shake the Kingdom from its back. Travellers tell tales of the great yawning holes that can open in an instant, on the forest paths, at the crossroads, or in the centre of the markets. They talk of how the Troll King was slain by the tumbling of the iron chain with which he bound his bride. They say his Sister paces the chambers of the World Below, driven mad with grief and she will not be at peace until she has swallowed up the whole Kingdom and every living soul within it.

ASHYPELT

Once there was a widowed Farmer and he had two sons. He ruled them in the same manner that he commanded his cattle – with stern speech and a strong stick. The beatings buckled the Eldest Son to obedience, but the Youngest Son was swift-footed and light-hearted and he made sport out of the dodging of his father's fists. The more the boy laughed at such attempts at correction, the more his father's heart hardened against him, until one day he cast his Youngest Son out of the house. He made his bed in the cinder pile in the yard, quite content with the warmth of the ashes beneath his back and the starlit wonders of the open sky above him. So it was that he earned his name – Ashypelt.

The years passed. The Eldest Son grew meeker by the month, but Ashypelt did not. They came to an easy agreement: sharing out their tasks according to their natures. The Eldest Son worked the cattle and the fields, always keeping within the enclosure of the farmstead fences. Ashypelt favoured adventure – the fetching of the wood from the depths of the forest, the breaking in of the bold stallion, the trapping of the wild rabbits. Nor did Ashypelt flinch from the striking of the slaughterknife and the skinning of flesh from fur. He cut quickly, keenly and with kindness.

The Eldest Son blanched to watch the bloody work and when the stew was set upon the table he could not swallow it.

'There is nothing in this world that holds one shudder of fear for you, brother Ashypelt,' he said. 'It is not natural in a man.'

That night as Ashypelt drew his dust-down blankets about his body, he turned his dear brother's words around in his mind. The more he considered the truth of them, the more he was determined. He would become a man. He would learn how to shudder with Fear.

At dawn the next day, Ashypelt set out in search of enlightenment.

The village Priest nodded, as Ashypelt told him of his dilemma. 'Indeed, a man without Fear in his heart is but half a man,' he said. 'However, your condition is simply a point of ignorance, my child.'

The Priest pulled out his sermon of brimstone and damnation. But the more Ashypelt heard of the fiery furnaces and the Devil's delight in torture and torment, the more he laughed.

'This is but the way of my own father's ruling writ in Church words,' he said. 'I have nothing to fear of the next world, if I am already accustomed to the tricks of it.'

The Priest steepled his hands into points of prayer as he considered Ashypelt's unfortunate interpretation. Here was a child who resided entirely in the physical realm, without any understanding of any form of spiritual responsibility or the life hereafter. Therefore, there was no alternative but to provide him with a direct education in the hope of saving the poor boy's soul.

Under the Priest's instruction, Ashypelt returned to the church at the strike of the midnight bell. The moon above was a scythe-splinter of light as he took the path to the charnel house. He felt out the shape of the cross carved upon the lintel of that bonebox.

The door swung open at his touch and closed tight shut behind. The air before him was as black as a pot of spilt ink.

But Ashypelt knew well enough from his dealings in the dark heart of the forest that when sight is stolen, other senses sharpen. He felt his way along the stacks of the pulled apart pieces of men. The clusters of thigh bones provided as sturdy a purchase as a tree-trunk trail, and he soon found himself standing before the skull shelf.

He recalled the Priest's precise request. 'A smooth-pated head, two handspans broad, without buckle or blemish.'

Ashypelt felt out the skulls as if he were sorting the apple harvest, separating the flawed from the fine, casting aside the cracked craniums until he clutched one unspoilt by injury. No sooner had he tucked the skull beneath his arm than a voice boomed at his back.

'That's my head, and it's not for taking!'

'Fair's fair,' laughed Ashypelt. 'I'll not carry away what's not given freely.'

He set the skull back down and resumed his bone-turning.

His fingertips met another smooth-browed specimen.

No sooner had he plucked it from its perch than the voice cried out again.

'That's my head, and it's not for taking!'

'Now then,' said Ashypelt, 'I've played true with you in this matter, Sir. I'll thank you to do the same by me.' He hooked his fingers into the skull sockets. 'No man, woman or child in this world is blessed with two heads.'

And with that, Ashypelt went marching out of the bonehouse.

He wedged a rock against the door, for he wasn't about to let any dishonest ghost come chasing at his heels, plucking his prize from him.

Then he set the skull at the threshold of the church door and went home whistling, thinking of how well he had followed every article of the Priest's instruction and how surely now he would be given the great gift of shuddering Fear as his reward.

Dawn was breaking when Ashypelt returned to the farm and made his bed of cinders. He slept soundly within it, untroubled by dreams.

He was woken by his father's boot upon his back and was kicked the length of the yard until he came to full standing.

'Idle wretch,' hollered the Farmer. 'Gallivanting the whole night through and slumbering the working day. Get you gone, for you are no son of mine.'

There was only one road ahead for Ashypelt, and it led to the place that awaits any man who finds himself turfed out of hearth and home at the borders of twilight.

Ashypelt slipped through the alehouse door and watched on from the shadows as all the men of the village first raised their flagons and then raised their fists and their voices.

They raged about how the Priest had been found stone-shuttered into the charnel house, struck dumb and shivering, his mind stripped clean of all scriptural certainty.

They declared as one – they would seek out the man responsible. He would be taken up to the tall tree on the high hill beyond the village boundary and there he would weep and he would shudder and he would be paid his dues.

Ashypelt listened and he smiled. Now he had the location where his Fear might be found. He had no need to burden this carousing company with the trouble of taking him to meet it.

The moon that rose above the hill was nothing but a fingernail fragment. As Ashypelt crested the brow, there emerging from the dappled dark was a triple-trunked tree, with stout, straight branches set between. Hanging from the branches was the strangest fruit Ashypelt had ever seen: stalks of tightly coiled, many-plaited hemp, bearing seven full-grown men, swinging and shuddering.

'My friends,' Ashypelt cried. 'I see that Fear has you in its grip and no mistake. Now tell me true, how might I gain an understanding equal to your own?'

The men gazed at him, blank-eyed and blue-lipped, and spoke no word of advice or instruction.

Ashypelt took the hand of the one nearest to him. It was cold to his touch.

'Forgive me,' said Ashypelt. 'You poor fellows are in clear need of more urgent assistance than myself.'

Ashypelt took the slaughterknife from his pocket and he cut the seven silent men from the stalks that held them, and lay them down upon the grass, side by side.

Then he set fists and feet to those triple trunks and beat against them until they broke. He untwisted the hemp, teased the strands out to tinder, staked the broken trunks on top of it, took the flintstone from his pocket and struck fire.

He put his seven companions close to the flames to warm them. Still they sat, staring and unspeaking.

Ashypelt stacked up the timber. The fire spat, a spark sprung onto the coat of one of the men, but he did not flinch. Neither did the fellow propped up beside him, nor the one at his shoulder, nor the next man as the flame jumped from back to back, as swift as thought.

Ashypelt leapt to his feet, rolled the seven bodies in the night-dewed grass and all were swiftly extinguished.

'Well,' said Ashypelt, 'if you've not got the wits or wisdom to save your own skins nor the good grace to thank me for my trouble, then you're of no help to me.'

Ashypelt turned his back upon the fire and walked on, leaving his silent companions to their several smouldering Fates.

Dawn was breaking once more as Ashypelt made his way down the hill, and it was a grey and desolate land that greeted him on the other side of it. No trees or flowers grew. The riverbank ran dry, and no birds sang. Still he followed the dusty path that unfolded beneath his feet as the day turned. As dusk was falling, it led him to the door of a castle of granite.

Carved upon the lintel of the door was a Phoenix, holding lines of lettering in the embrace of its flame-feathers.

> *BOLD TRAVELLER, VENTURE YOU NO*
> *FURTHER HERE*
> *LEST YOUR BLOOD RUN COLD WITH FEAR.*

Ashypelt stepped swiftly across the threshold.

There in the hallway beyond stood twelve guardsmen, their hands upon the hilts of their swords. Opposite them, twelve maidservants, with silken handkerchiefs set before their faces.

In the centre of this gathered company stood the most beautiful woman Ashypelt had ever seen. Her skin was milk-white, her hair raven-black and her lips as red as blood. She gazed upon Ashypelt, and her blue eyes showed neither kindness nor cruelty. She was dressed in robes of red velvet and there was a golden crown upon her head.

Ashypelt bowed deeply.

'Forgive my bold intrusion, Your Majesty,' he said. 'But I come, in accordance with the inscription of your Royal crest, in the most earnest pursuit of Fear.'

Still she gazed down, expressionless.

Then Ashypelt understood the truth of the matter. This courtly company was a perfectly painted deception. Hewn from the same grey stone of the castle, dressed and decorated to create a cunningly carved illusion of protection.

The castle walls rang with Ashypelt's laughter at the clever trick of it as he strode through the stone-bound company and into the great chamber beyond. It was a grand hall, with an empty hearth as wide as the triple-barred gate of the farmyard.

On one side of the hearth stood a fine four-poster bed, treetop tall and the breadth of five feeding troughs. On the other side, a table, three furrows wide and the height of a haywagon, laid out with a banquet – bread and meats and cheese and wine, piled up to heaving. Ashypelt felt his belly churn with a hunger he had not known he was carrying.

But no sooner had Ashypelt begun to shin his way up the table leg, than there came a rumbling from the chimney stack. Behind the rumbling came a tumbling as hurtling down into the hearth came a walloping wide waist, with a giant pair of legs attached, sporting leather breeches and boots with hobnails the size of loaf tins that sparked against the flagstones as they kicked themselves to standing.

'Well met, my friend!' cried Ashypelt. 'I do believe that you and I are of the same stock. Half-men both, for I am sure a fine fellow like yourself has never felt one shudder of Fear.'

No sooner had Ashypelt spoken than the chimney let out a great roar and down plummeted a chest as broad as three barrels, with arms, neck and a huge hulking head on top.

The arms stirred up an ash storm as they clawed their way out. They scuttled over to the sure-standing legs, and with a push, sprung up on top, fitting at the waist like the stoppering up of the cider flagon with a stout cork.

There, staring down at Ashypelt, was a buckle-browed iron-eyed Giant, with a mouth as wide as an oven door and a long lolling tongue that licked about his blood-crusted lips as he spoke.

'If it's Fear you're after then it's Fear you'll get,' bellowed the Giant. 'Before the night is through you shall shudder so sorely that your very soul will be shaken from your body and I'll have both for the taking.'

'Thank you kindly,' said Ashypelt. 'That's just the kind of adventure I'm after.'

The Giant roared again, but this time with laughter. The foundations of the castle shook. Behind that shaking there came a rattling and a rolling as a jangling jumble of bones came toppling down the chimney.

The Giant plucked them from the hearth, as if he were pulling apart a set of matchsticks. As Ashypelt watched on, he saw that these were articles he knew from the charnel house: the long, flesh-stripped thigh bones of men.

The Giant placed the thigh bones at the far end of the hall, in a tight triangle – five, by three, by two, by one – the same arrangement as the setting of the skittles in the alehouse yard. Then the Giant went to the hearth once more and pulled out a pair of skulls. He took one for himself and gave the other to Ashypelt.

'One strike for one soul!' he declared.

Before Ashypelt could say a word against the wager, the Giant set the skull spinning. Crown over socket over bone-fixed grin it went rolling, and struck swift and sure. Nine thighs collapsed, clattering. One lurched and listed but did not fall.

The Giant was at the skittle stack in a single stride.

Ashypelt ran his hand across the crooked cranium of his skull-ball and thought of his good friend the Priest and his insistence on the smooth-pated perfection of his prize.

'There's no fair wager in a loaded dice or a crooked billet,' said Ashypelt to himself.

As the Giant reset the arrangement – five, by three, by two, by one – Ashypelt took the slaughterknife from his pocket and set the blade to the bone and whittled away the unevenness. Then he threw.

The flagstones sung as bone chimed against bone. The moment all ten skeleton skittles fell with the striking of the skull they turned to dust.

The Giant howled. Chest fell from legs, legs kicked chest to the hearth and both went scrabbling up the chimney and were gone.

Ashypelt raced after.

'Fair's fair, Sir!' he cried. 'I agreed to your wager, now you must honour it. Full payment of the sure shudder of Fear.'

But there was no reply, only the echo of his own voice returning from the hollow hearth.

Fear... Fear... Fear...

Ashypelt scaled up to the heights of the Giant's table and he feasted until he was full, but he took no pleasure in it. Then with a heavy heart, Ashypelt made his way to his hearthside bed.

He climbed the curtains and swung himself onto the mountain of the mattress. Where the featherdown pillows and silken sheets should have been there was a wooden box, the dimension of a man's body. A coffin casket.

Ashypelt prised open the lid and there lay his own dear Elder Brother, eyes closed, hands folded across his chest.

'How foolish I have been!' Ashypelt cried, 'to seek my adventure elsewhere, when surely there is no man in the world that has a truer understanding of the shudders of Fear than my own kin.'

His Elder Brother gave neither a flicker of recognition nor a word of reply.

Ashypelt pulled him into his embrace. He was as cold as clay to the touch.

Ashypelt thought of how it would take but a second of stout stamping and splitting to cast that coffin to firewood. Furthermore, what a lesson it would be to that dishonest Giant to smoke him out of his hiding place and demand his dues.

But although Ashypelt was fearless, he was not foolish. He had learned the lesson of the high hill. He would not risk the singeing of one hair on his dear brother's head for the pursuit of his own purpose.

Ashypelt climbed into the coffin and held his Elder Brother close, in the hope that warmth would bring wakefulness.

It began with the tingling of the tip of Ashypelt's little finger, where it sat resting against his dear brother's heart.

Then he felt the flesh beneath his touch shifting.

Fists and feet swelled fat and fierce, the brow buckled and an iron eye winked open.

Ashypelt sprung from the coffin bed and shoved the lid down fast.

He carved the charnel house cross at the head and foot, then sat upon the coffin top and held on tight.

The thing inside the coffin, part Giant, part stuck in his magic-made man-skin, howled and hurled and set the box tipping.

Ashypelt rode that coffin-caught creature up and down the length of the hall, kicking at the belly of it with his heels, laughing as he did so.

Back and forth they went, clattering and cursing, buckling and braying the whole night through until, cutting through the cacophony, there came another sound from the world beyond the castle walls: the thrice-throated call of the cockerel.

The coffin casket stilled and ceased.

'The night is done, the wager's won,' said Ashypelt. 'Now let's be having the promised and proper payment of shuddering Fear.'

He clambered off the coffin and lifted the lid.

There was nothing inside but a pile of ashes.

But within that dowry of dust and dirt, something stirred.

There was an amber eye, staring up at him.

Then in a flurry of golden feathers, a Phoenix unfolded and flew, faster than firelight, up the chimney and was gone.

Then the door of the hall opened and there was the Queen.

No longer statue-bound, her beauty burned brighter still as she walked towards Ashypelt and knelt at his feet.

In soft, sweet speech she told of the Giant who had come to claim her as his bride and of the enchantment set upon her and her company when she refused him.

She told of the noble Princes who had come before him and their Fear-frozen, soul-stripped Fates – reduced to their skeleton selves, the Giant's playthings.

She told how Ashypelt's kindness, courage and cunning had broken the enchantment, and with that breaking, her heart was his.

The Queen took the golden crown from her head and offered it up.

'For there are no truer qualities than those three,' she said, 'in the character of a King.'

The guardsmen and the maidservants came crowding into the grand hall, echoing the gesture of their mistress: kneeling, heads bowed and hands clasped before them, in anticipation of service.

Ashypelt thought of the machinations of majesty.

The setting out of the laws of how a man might live and the meting out of punishment for those who broke them.

The battles and the bloodshed.

The sacrifice of his own dreams and desires in favour of the trappings of a title.

He felt a fist of ice clenching around the chambers of his heart.

A cold sweat came creeping across his skin.

Then the shuddering began.

JUST JIMMY

O nce there was a man who could not tell a lie. His name was Just Jimmy, and he was born with the skill of fixing in his blood. The moment he set eyes upon a thing that was broken, his palms would be itching with the need to put it right.

Jimmy was broad-backed and strong-shouldered. He had hair as red as firelight, but his temper did not match it. He was fair-minded and he was gentle with it. He'd never set a price beyond true reckoning, nor spin out a day's labour for a week of payment. He worked hard and he worked honest.

In Springtime he would be found out at the edges of the fields, setting fenceposts to keep the curious calves from the cliffside. At Midsummer he would be sat in the market square, striking hammer to hobnail on the boots of the men setting out for the long roads. When Autumn came, he would be on the roof of the inn, twister and pins in hand, working the thatch, securing good cheer for all when Winter rolled round.

There are the truths that folk thank a man for speaking, and then there are the ones they do not. When Jimmy spat watered-down ale across the flagstones, the Innkeeper cursed him for the loss of patronage and profit that followed. It went the same way for the travelling Merchant, when Jimmy stood in the market square with a shattered tooth in his upturned hand, telling of the harsh bite of falsely coined gold. And it went even worse for the poor Farmer. When Jimmy pulled the posey from his own pocket, wrapped in the lace-latticed handkerchief of the Farmer's dear wife, he might just as well have cut the horns from the cattle and fashioned them into a cuckold's crown.

It was not long before the voice of three men became the voice of the village. For who can trust a worker who takes folks' secrets for currency to spend however he sees fit?

So Jimmy put his pack upon his back and set out. But no matter how far across the land he travelled, he found that it went the same. Folk welcomed true craftsmanship, but not the true speech that came with it. Often as not, they would match his honesty with false payment – or no payment at all.

Jimmy walked away all the trappings of his trade, until his boots were broken, his coat torn to tatters and his tools rusted to useless.

On the first of May, heartsore and footsore, Jimmy came to a village. There on the green was a mass of folk, gathered around a freshly hewn whetstone. Jimmy felt his luck about to turn. Surely he could trade a favour of sharpening for work paid back in kind?

Then the Inkeeper stepped forward and his challenge sounded across the air.
  'He who has the sharpest wit is worthy of the sharpest knives. So let the best and boldest liar claim this fine whetstone as his prize!'

Jimmy walked away across paddock and pasture, field and forest, until he came to the edge of a wide lake. He looked out to the far shore beyond which twisted and shimmered on the horizon – sometimes there, sometimes not.

Tethered to a post, half-hidden in the shallows, was a rowing boat. One oar set true upon its fixing. The other, lagging against a loosened thole, so that the vessel circled slow widdershins around its mooring.

Jimmy's palms itched. He undid his pack and took out his woodknife. The boat lurched against the bulk of his body as he set his foot upon it. Up was down, down was up; the water above him, the sky below. Jimmy tumbled into the hollow hull and all was blackness.

Jimmy woke to find himself drifting on a sea of stars, the prow of the little boat churning the reflected moon. He sat himself up and rubbed the back of his head. There was a lumpen swelling, as plump as a peach. But that was not all there was.

The hair that met his fingers was long and fine. Jimmy scratched his chin. Where his bristled beard should have been, he found himself stroking smooth skin. He looked down at his hands. They were soft, slender and unspoiled, bearing no sign of hard labour. Slowly, with a trembling touch, he felt out his own shape. All that had been stout and sturdy was now the opposite.

Jimmy gazed into the moonlit mirror of the lake. He was clad in a white silken gown, well suited to the pale beauty that stared back at him, wide-eyed in the water. It was impossible, and yet it was the truth. Jimmy was a woman.

Jimmy sat silent, transfixed by the sight of this new, unknown self. The boat lurched beneath her, unaided by her touch, and went forwards and onwards towards the other shore.

The dawn was bleeding across the sky when Jimmy beached up on a ridge of white sand. Beyond there was a forest and a single path through it. She stuck her woodknife in the belt of her dress and walked on.

Jimmy was not far into the forest when there was a crashing in the undergrowth, and stumbling out onto the path ahead came a White Stag with golden antlers.

Jimmy looked at it, it looked at Jimmy, and an understanding passed between them. Then it bolted and was gone.

Then there was the call of a hunting horn and thundering down the path came a bold black stallion. On its back was a handsome young man dressed in red livery, with a sword swinging at his side.

'Have you seen a fine White Stag pass this way?' he cried.

'That I have,' said Jimmy.

For a moment she was silenced by the sweetness of her own voice, and then she found it again.

'And if any harm comes to that White Stag, whatever it is that you love most in all the world will be forever lost to you.'

'So I have heard tell,' scoffed the young man. 'From the mouths of Henwives and Simpletons. It is only a story.'

'That's as maybe,' said Jimmy. 'But some stories are true.'

The young man halted then, and looked at Jimmy as if he was seeing her for the first time.

'What is your name?' he said.

'Just Jimmy,' she replied.

'That's a cruel name to give a beautiful maiden.'

'It is the name my father had before me and his father also,' said Jimmy.

The young man scratched his head.

'And where have you come from?' he asked.

'From a place where I was not welcome,' Jimmy replied.

'And where are you headed to?'

'That I do not know,' said Jimmy. 'I am entirely lost.'

The young man smiled and there was a kindness about him as he did so.

'Well then,' he said, 'now you are found.'

Before Jimmy could protest, the young man leapt from his horse, scooped Jimmy up in his arms, placed her on the saddle, sat himself behind her, grabbed hold of the reins and turned his horse about. They went galloping down that forest path together, until it came to the gate of a grand castle.

There they were met by guardsmen, who bowed low before the young man and stared directly at Jimmy. She understood the truth of the matter then. Whatever this land was, this bold young huntsman was Prince of it.

The Prince led Jimmy to the castle kitchen where scowling servants placed food before her.

'I'm grateful for the kindness,' she said. 'But I've never taken charity from prince or pauper and I'll not be changing that now.'

So it was that Jimmy went to work in the Royal kitchens. She slept by the fireside on her bed of straw and cinders with her woodknife beneath her pillow and she kept that blade sharp.

Years passed and Jimmy's story went the way that these tales do. The Prince fell in love with the strange young woman who was as honest as she was beautiful and over time she came to love him also. They married, and to Jimmy's great surprise and joy they had three daughters.

The Eldest Daughter had her father's dark hair and strong laughter. The Middle Daughter was fair and had her mother's pale skin and sweet voice. The Youngest Daughter had hair as red as sunset and a clever and curious mind. She was happiest in the Royal stables, pulling apart reins and bridle and then piecing them together again to understand their workings. Jimmy loved Bold Red best of all, but she did not speak that truth to anyone.

One bright Spring morning, Jimmy was woken by the sound of crying and commotion. Bold Red was missing, and so was her fine pony. The Prince called his best huntsmen to him and they all rode out into the forest together. But the paths that Jimmy knew so well seemed to twist and turn against her that day and she soon found herself where she had been years before – lost and alone in the dark heart of the woods.

She called out for her Youngest Daughter until she had no voice left.

And then, the forest answered.

'Mother! Mother, help me!'

Jimmy turned her steed towards the call and followed it until she came to a clearing, all gloom and shadow.

There was the pony, lame and limping.

There, lying on the ground beside it, was Bold Red.

And there, standing above her dearest daughter, Jimmy

could make out the shape of a horned beast, hoof set upon her heart.

A mother's instinct is quicker than thought. Jimmy pulled her woodknife from her belt and she threw it. The blade pierced the flank and stuck. The creature turned, its golden horns glinting, and Jimmy saw it for what it really was.

The White Stag looked at Jimmy, Jimmy looked at it, and an understanding passed between them.

Then it bolted and was gone.

When Jimmy turned her gaze back to the forest floor, Bold Red was not there.

Jimmy chased the blood trail. She pushed through thornbush and thicket until her Royal robes were torn to tatters and she came stumbling out at the edge of the lake. There was the rowing boat rocking gently in the shallows with the sand stained red before it.

Jimmy leapt inside, but the boat was empty. She staggered and she slipped, and then all was blackness.

When Jimmy woke, she could hear shouts and laughter echoing down the wind. It was the sound of celebration and feasting.

Jimmy ran up the shoreline, across forest and field, pasture and paddock, until she came to a village green.

'My daughter!' she cried. 'My husband! Are they amongst you?'

The crowd all turned to Jimmy and stood silent as she told her tale. She told of the Prince she loved and of their youngest and dearest, Bold Red, so eager for adventures beyond her years. She told of the White Stag and of the warning that it carried in its eyes. She told of the quick flight of her sharp woodknife and everything that came after.

When Jimmy finished her story, the crowd applauded as one.

The Innkeeper strode forward.

'Of all this fine company I do declare,' he cried, 'the Most Absolute Liar Therein and let none of you contest it.'

Jimmy looked down at her hand as she set it on the stone.

The fingertips were crowned with calluses, the knuckles were cracked and the nails were black-rimmed and broken. And there, sprouting on the back of the hand, running up the length of the arm, was thick red hair.

Just Jimmy's tears flowed down his cheeks and salted his beard as he wept.

In the Other Land, the Prince also wept as he followed the path of blood out of the forest and onto the wide white sand. There he saw a single line of slender footprints leading down to the water and none returning.

The Prince went to his castle and locked the strong gate. He placed his two remaining daughters in the tallest tower and kept their door guarded day and night. The forest, untended, grew quickly. The paths were swallowed up; the thickets and thornbushes crept all around the walls, tangling the turrets.

But as for Bold Red, who lost her mother yet found her freedom, this is just the start of her story.

LITTLE SPARROW

O nce there was a Woodcutter and he had a Wife. They made their home in a cottage by the forest and there they lived and loved together well. It was not long before they had a child. She came into the world laughing and as she grew to girlhood her nature did not change. She had a lightness in her heart, a quickness in her step and she went through her days dancing. So it was that they came to call her Little Sparrow.

Some folk are allotted their full span of joyful years. For others the thread of life is cut cruelly short. As Little Sparrow's seventh Summer rolled round, a great weight of sadness and slowness settled upon the heart and bones of the Woodcutter's Wife. As the roses blossomed in the hedgerows, her skin grew as pale as the sheets upon the bed that she could no longer rise from.

She called her daughter to her.

'Little Sparrow,' she said. 'There are two sides to all things. The old must make way for the new. As sure sunrise follows sunset, this world is made for turning. Let not your heart turn to sorrow with it.'

With that she kissed her daughter and gave into her care two treasures. The gifts that her dear husband had presented on their wedding day: a golden comb and a shawl of blue silk.

Then she closed her eyes and did not open them again.

As the world turned around Little Sparrow, she saw the truth of her mother's words. Beneath the quick green grass of the graveyard lay cold dark earth.

The soil had not long settled when Little Sparrow saw that there was another other side to her father, also.

The whole village came out in ceremony for the Woodcutter's second wedding. For there was not one corner of the market square, the threshing barn or the alehouse that his tale had not travelled to. The story of the Lost Princess he had found wandering in the dark heart of the forest, without any knowledge of her name or the land from whence she came. The village folk spoke of how, as surely as heads chase tails, love could be cast like a coin. Little Sparrow's mother was a bold, black-haired beauty and her daughter the very echo of her. But his new love was blessed with a grace that was opposite and yet equal. It was as if she had been pieced together from flowers that blossomed across the wild woodland at Springtime, with her eyes of forget-me-not blue, daisy-white skin and hair the colour of the bright bonny yellow broom. They spoke of how there was no better man worthy of such a blessing, no daughter more deserving to be so twice-loved.

But that was not the way things went for Little Sparrow.

The moment her father placed his axe in his belt and strode out of the door whistling, her sweet Stepmother swiftly soured and showed her other side. She set Little Sparrow to all the hard tasks of the house – and as she worked, her Stepmother was always at her elbow, pinching and poking.

Each night the Woodcutter returned it was the same story – his woodland Wife fed him lies alongside sweet slices of honeycake, claiming his dear daughter's work as her own. She told him tales of the tiresome trouble of Little Sparrow, who slouched and sulked about the house, without one word of kindness or care for her new mother.

Her wicked words wove their way into first his mind and then his heart. He looked upon his daughter and he saw indeed how changed she was. Her shoulders were stooped, her face was clouded with a dark frown and when she had once danced through her days, she now dragged sullen footsteps.

The more he looked, the more he had no doubt it was the sharp tongue and sour temper of Little Sparrow that had curdled the milk, turned the honey to vinegar and the sugar to salt. So when the evening came that his new Wife banished his blighted daughter from the house, with but a dry crust of burnt bread for her supper, he did not raise one word of protest.

Little Sparrow sought shelter in the timber shed. As she laid herself down to sleep, there was a scrabbling beside her and out of the woodstack hopped a scruff-coated Mousekin.

She placed the burnt bread beside him. He took it between his paws, broke it in two and they shared it.

'Fear not, Little Sparrow,' said the Mousekin. 'This is not the fixing of your Fate.'

Little Sparrow remembered her True Mother's words. As the Mousekin nestled down to sleep at her shoulder she kept determined hold of her own heart and did not let her sorrow sink it.

Little Sparrow woke with the dawn, at the slam of the cottage door. She spied silently as the Woodcutter strode forestwards without as much as a backwards glance – as if he had forgotten that he ever had a daughter.

She looked down; there was her Mousekin burrowing back into the woodpile.

She looked up; there was her Stepmother.

'The time has come for you to set your idle bones to use, my girl,' said she. 'Get you gone into the forest. Follow the toppled trees to the home of my sister. Ask her directly for the needle and thread best suited to your particular purpose and she will give you what is your due.'

There came a cold curdling deep in the heart of Little Sparrow as she thought that out there, in the depth of the dark woods, there might be another woman who shared the blood and nature of her savage Stepmother – and that she was waiting.

But morning is wiser than the evening.

If this was the task that she must be given, then what use was there in arguing against it?

'I would go gladly, Mother dearest,' said Little Sparrow. 'All I ask is a bannock baked with your blessing to send me on my way.'

Whilst her Stepmother busied herself at the stove, Little Sparrow ran to her bed, pulled the blue shawl and the golden comb from beneath her pillow and shoved them deep into her apron pocket.

Her Stepmother gave her a linen-bound bundle of bread, still warm to the touch. Little Sparrow thanked her for her kindness and set out on the forest paths.

The pine trees clustered in on all sides, those barbed branches ranging up above her head as if they were scratching out the sky. Little Sparrow had heard tales of the dizzying darkness of the wild woods, and the way they robbed all sense of purpose or direction from any soul who ventured inwards. She had thought her father was the only man who could not be caught by the enchantments of that place, but now she understood that he was not.

She called out for her father again and again, but it was as if those spikes and spines skewered the flight of her words, caging all sound and thought.

Still, onward and deeper she went.

But then, the path turned, sharp and sudden. The trees before her lay fallen.

Little Sparrow could not remember a time when she did not know the ways of reading wood. She could tell the metal of a blade from a single bark stroke. She could tell the nature of every wild animal by the cut of tooth and claw.

Whatever had toppled these trees was neither.

The trunks were torn apart, their innards chewed to pith. The fir tips were cast as sure and straight and true as a flight of arrows, urging her directly onwards, and in.

Fear and hunger rolled and roiled against each other in her belly.

Little Sparrow unbound the bannock-bundle from her back, pulled her mother's shawl from her pocket and set it upon the ground.

A scorching cascade of oven-baked stones struck the silk.

The sorrow that Little Sparrow had so long set aside came rising up in a great wave.

Then there was a scrabbling and scratching beside her.

'Fear not, Little Sparrow, this is not the fixing of your Fate.'

The Mousekin jumped from a bark-burrowed hole onto her shoulder.

'Look again at what lies before you.'

There she saw where her stone supper had lain was now a feast of bread, jam and honeycakes.

They shared it all out even and equal, and as they feasted Little Sparrow told of her Stepmother's instructions of needle and thread and the pursuit of her sister.

The Mousekin stood and sniffed the air, testing the four corners of the wind.

'Let not folly falter your footsteps,' he said. 'Whatever comes to meet you look at it directly, and do not fear it.'

And with that he scampered back beneath the toppled tree trunk and was gone.

Little Sparrow shook the crumbs from the shawl, tucked it back into her pocket and followed the direction of those tree posts, inwards and onwards.

She walked but seven paces when there, stuck upon a brambled bush, was a blue ribbon. She remembered the advice of her wise Mousekin and she took the ribbon in her hands.

She looked at it directly, wondering at the tale it might tell. Of what might have become of another girl who had taken this turning before her. She put the ribbon in her pocket and went on.

Seven more paces and the path beneath her feet was grabbing and grappling at her ankles, a sudden quagmire crossing. Then beneath her slippered foot, the strong edge of something. She reached down into the puddle depths and there was a bottle blown from blue glass stoppered with a strong cork. She wiped away the dirt and there she saw, slicking up the side of it, oil.

She wondered at the tale it might tell. Of what might have become of the Woodcutter, Soldier or Vagabond who had found himself lost in the heart of the forest without the means of sharpening his instruments. She pressed that cork down tight, put the bottle in her pocket and went on.

Seven more paces and at the edge of the undergrowth was a flash of white, shimmering and shining. She slowed her pace and kept her gaze fixed upon the road ahead. She had heard the tales of the lantern lights that call to the lost travellers, leading them away from the sure path and into the grey gaps of the world, never to return.

But then as she neared, she saw it for what it really was. A white silk handkerchief caught upon the bracken. She folded that handkerchief foursquare, put it in her pocket and went on.

Seven more paces and the forest-folded gloom before her rose up and thickened into a solid thing – a stewing black cloud that swirled and hummed and settled upon her skin. A fetid fly storm, fierce and furious.

There, upon the path before her, Little Sparrow saw the cause of it: a loaf of mouldering bread and a pile of rancid meat.

She knew their story well enough – she had heard the tales of the unwanted children and the trails and tracks they left in the hope of return.

She bound the bread and meat inside her mother's shawl and walked on.

Seven more paces and the trees seemed to be shifting and parting at her footsteps.

Suddenly, she was standing in a clearing, and she understood then the nature of her Stepmother's instruction.

Before her stood a fence of flesh-flayed bones and those bones were human.

There were lattice links of thigh and shin; arm-anchored prop posts, each crowned by a grinning skull. The gate was a ratcheted rack of ribs, fastened with a lock of tethered teeth.

By the gate there was a well and beside it stood a broad birch tree, branches bent to the dust and the sound of the wind through their leaves was the sound of weeping.

Little Sparrow took the ribbon from her pocket and tied back the tree.

With the binding of the birch, she saw what lay beyond that bone boundary.

There stood a stout-stilted shack of torn-apart timber.

A dog half the height of a horse, with starve-patched fur, was running rings around it. As the dog barked and bolted, the shack listed like a ship upon a roiling sea. The stilts were not stilts at all, but scrabbling scaled hen's legs and the dog was nipping at their heels, setting the house spinning.

Little Sparrow gathered her courage.

The moment she set her hand upon the bone gate the lock of teeth screamed and snapped at her fingers.

She took the bottle from her pocket, pooled the oil into her palm and eased it into each and every blemished bone.

The ribs sighed as she rubbed them smooth. The jaw unclenched and the gate swung open before her.

The dog turned away from the hounding of the hen's legs and fixed its wild-eyed gaze upon Little Sparrow.

She unbound the shawl and there inside was a fresh loaf of bread.

The dog took it from her outstretched hand, tail wagging.

The claws of the hen's legs dug into the dirt. The house ceased its spinning and stood firm as Little Sparrow clambered up across the threshold.

The parlour room she tumbled into was dark and uncertain. From the corner, two green eyes stared out at her. There was a spitting and hissing and a bristle-backed bony black cat separated itself from the shadows.

The meat that Little Sparrow took from the shawl was now charmed sweet and tender. The cat took it from her outstretched hand, purring and pawing.

At the far side of the room was a bone-bolted strong door. Little Sparrow slipped the knuckle-latch and went through it.

There was a hearth the height of the house, with a great iron barrel of an oven set in the heart of it. Standing beside that oven was a stoop-shouldered, soot-smeared girl and she was weeping.

Little Sparrow took the handkerchief from her pocket and pressed it into the girl's hand.

The girl's mouth twisted into something like a smile. It was as if she was wrestling with a wealth of words, but she did not utter a single one.

Then the floor of the cottage began to shake and there came the sound of steel striking against steel. Little Sparrow saw that set on the walls of that kitchen were racks of hooks and nails, and swinging from them were sharp-bladed knives, spiked skewers and pots of every depth and dimension – all chiming.

Then the door flew back on its hinges and there stood a bony-legged old woman dressed in black, with hair as grey as spun steel and skin as sallow as saddle leather. Her chin buckled upwards, and her nose hooked downwards to meet it. She turned her gaze upon Little Sparrow. Her eyes were as red as burning coals.

'Well, my pretty,' said the old woman, 'what brings you to my kitchen, so bold and unbidden?'

She grinned as she spoke. Her teeth were spikes of iron.

The moment Little Sparrow looked upon the old woman she knew her.

For every child in the village had heard the tales, whispered by fireside through the nights of the long dark Winters. Tales of enchantments and entrapment, boiling and bone-grinding. And here was the terrible truth of them, standing before her.

The wild witch of the woods – Baba Yaga.

Little Sparrow bowed her head.

'I beg pardon and I mean no harm,' she said. 'But only the asking of a simple favour.'

Baba Yaga's grin twisted wider and sharper.

'Not all questions bring good,' she said. 'Better young and happy be, than to pluck the apple from the tree.'

Little Sparrow remembered the words of her Mousekin. She looked directly at Baba Yaga and she did not falter.

'The question is not mine to leave unspoken,' she said. 'Your own sister sent me to fetch a needle and thread, best suited to my own particular purpose.'

Baba Yaga grinned so wide it seemed her skin might split with the stretching of it. 'Then a needle and thread you shall have, my niece.'

Baba Yaga scrabbled at her scalp and pulled out a long snaking hair. Then she gnawed at the little finger of her left hand, flaying the flesh, snapping it at the root and piercing the end of it.

She grinned once more, bold and bloodied, as she offered up the steel thread and the bone-bitten needle.

Little Sparrow kept tight hold of her courage as she took Baba Yaga's gifts and thanked her for them.

'Favour is as favour does,' said Baba Yaga.

She placed her hand upon Little Sparrow's elbow, the bloodied stump of her finger already sprouting new growth as she pulled Little Sparrow backwards into the parlour.

She lit a candle and there Little Sparrow saw a loom set in the cat's corner, with the warp and the weft knitted into a cradle of knots.

'Work away and weave, my pretty niece,' said Baba Yaga. 'And I'll see to the fetching of wood and water and the setting of the supper.'

The words were spoken sweetly, but Little Sparrow knew well enough the meaning held at the heart of them.

'That I will, Auntie,' she said. 'And gladly.'

Baba Yaga returned to the kitchen. Little Sparrow took her place at the loom.

She pulled the golden comb from her pocket, set it to the thread and all that was caught crooked ran swiftly true.

The shuttle of that loom was a shaven shinbone. Little Sparrow's hand trembled as she shot it back and forth, forth and back, clacking and clattering.

The cat came pawing at her ankles.

'Tell me true,' said the cat. 'If there was a way out of this, would you take it?'

'That I would,' said Little Sparrow.

'Well then,' said the cat, 'I will help you.'

With the next flight of the shinbone it was the cat's claw, not the hand of Little Sparrow, that caught it.

As quick as thought or firelight, Little Sparrow was the out of the window, across the dirt yard, through the gate and beneath the birch tree.

There was the servant girl at the well.

Not one word passed between them but Little Sparrow saw there in her hand it was not a pitch pail she was setting to the water, but a stout steel sieve.

The forest beyond rang with the sound of teeth tearing treetops.

Little Sparrow ran as fast as she could away from all of it.

Baba Yaga straddled the broken-barked iron-eaten toppled tree trunk and rode it back to the door of her shack. There was the clackety-clack of her bone loom.

'Work and weave, my pretty niece,' she cried. 'And we shall feast well tonight.'

'That I will, Auntie,' called the cat. 'And gladly.'

Baba Yaga was through the window in an instant, for she knew well enough that mannered mewling was a far cry from the sweet-songed voice of Little Sparrow. There she saw the loom all knot-tangled once more, with her cat sat beside it, grinning.

Baba Yaga kicked her from the stool.

'You know your place and purpose,' she cried. 'And yet you did not scratch my supper-sent niece's eyes out.'

The cat spat back in kind.

'You have kept me lean for hunting all these years. What favour is held by cruelty when weighed against kindness?'

Baba Yaga flew raging out into the dirt yard.

There was the dog, sat licking his paws by the open gate of teeth and bone.

'You know your place and purpose, both,' cried Baba Yaga. 'Gates, why did you not cage-catch her? Dog, why did you not bite her into pieces?'

'You hunger-held me and set me to herd and hound with no reward but crumbs from your table,' said the dog. 'What favour is held by cruelty when weighed against kindness?'

The gate grinned in agreement.

'There are two sides to the nature of a lock,' said the gate. 'There is the forcing, or the freeing. You set our various parts against each other, with no care for the pain of such binding. What favour is held by cruelty when weighed against kindness?'

Baba Yaga kicked aside the dog and wrenched the gate from its haunch-hinges as she flew through it.

There was the birch tree, the well and the serving girl beside it.

'You know your place and purpose, both,' cried Baba Yaga.

'Tree, why did you not beat her back? Girl, why did you not duck and drown her?'

'You kept me bent and buckled, for your own purpose of cruelty and concealment,' sighed the birch tree. 'But she bound me with beauty so that I might stand true. What favour is held by cruelty when weighed against kindness?'

The servant girl unstooped her shoulders.

'You ruled me with torment and it's many the poor soul I have offered up to your cruel cooking pot for the sake of saving my own skin,' she said. 'But she showed me care and kindness and you shall not have her.'

At these words, Baba Yaga flew at the serving girl, teeth grinding and howling.

But the birch tree opened up its arms and gathered her up into the highest branches.

'Foolish and faithless servants,' cried Baba Yaga. 'I shall fetch what is my due, and upon my returning the worse it shall go for you.'

Little Sparrow was racing down the twisted tracks at the heart of the forest when she felt the ground beneath her feet begin to shake as if the land itself was buckling to throw her from its back.

Then she felt a scrabbling at her shoulder and the voice that whispered into her ear was a voice she knew.

'Now comes the fixing of your Fate,' said the Mousekin. 'As it goes in your world, so it is in the land of Baba Yaga. There are two sides to all things. Love runs lightly as hate holds hard.'

And with that, the Mousekin was gone.

The thundering of the land grew stronger and Little Sparrow felt each and every bone in her body shake with it.

She turned and looked behind her.

There was a great cloud of dust and dirt hurtling down the path and Baba Yaga was at the heart of it. She was riding her pestle and mortar, grinding the stone stump against the belly of the bowl with one hand as she urged it onwards. In her other hand she had her besom broom and was sweeping the tracks before her.

The forest rang with iron-edged laughter as she gained her ground.

Little Sparrow thought of the Mousekin's words.

She took her mother's shawl and she threw it down upon the path.

The moment silk met scrub soil it began to swell and shift its softness. There was a deep blue river, running fierce and foaming.

The pestle and mortar were pounding at such a pace that Baba Yaga had not the chance to still them.

The stone that had shown a savage strength upon the land was a weakness in the water and Baba Yaga's chariot sank beneath her.

But Baba Yaga held on fast to her besom broom as the tide turned against her.

She twisted open her mouth, stretching flesh, tooth and bone back upon itself and she swallowed up the whole of that raging river in one gulp.

There on the riverbed path was her pestle and mortar. She leapt inside, struck the stone, set her broom before her and hurtled on.

In the deep heart of the forest the trees on all sides began to tremble, as if the Fear running through Little Sparrow's blood was stewing their sap in sympathy.

Little Sparrow took her mother's comb and she threw it down upon the path.

The moment gold teeth met grey ground the tines began to twist. They burrowed deep into the earth and scrambled up the sky. There was a burnished briar bush set suddenly between Little Sparrow and Baba Yaga.

Baba Yaga stilled her pestle and mortar, flung aside her broom and leapt down laughing.

'Fine-fleshed and foolish faithful, niece of mine,' she cried. 'Soft gold is no match for iron will.'

And she twisted her mouth open once more.

Love runs lightly. Hate holds hard.

Baba Yaga bit at the golden bracken with all her might. It sighed and shifted around her, dancing, and pulled Baba Yaga into its shining embrace.

Little Sparrow ran and ran until she came to the edge of the forest, and there was her cottage beside it.

She stepped across the threshold. Her Stepmother and her father were sat beside the fire.

'Little Sparrow,' her father scolded, 'is there no end to your wickedness? Running out into the forest and leaving your new mother witless with worry. For what possible purpose?'

'Be wary of such questions,' said Little Sparrow. 'They do not bring good.'

She pulled the bone needle from her pocket and gazed directly at her Stepmother through the eye of it and she saw her for what she really was.

The golden hair withered to greyness, the blue eyes burned red and the skin sallowed. The Stepmother's nose hooked downwards and her chin buckled up to meet it – and set betwixt the two was a grin of iron teeth.

Little Sparrow took the hair of steel and threaded the hag-bone hole.

All that had been hidden inside turned outwards.

The skin of the Stepmother's spell split asunder and there she stood in her true twisted glory.

Baba Yaga's Sister let out a scream that shook the walls and the world beyond them, then in a single leap she was out of the window and running flailing through the forest.

The Woodcutter wept as he heard of how the gifts of his own true love had saved his Little Sparrow. The golden comb and the blue silk shawl. As well as the other gifts of his lost Wife's nature, her kindness and her courage that his own dearest daughter carried in her heart. And he wept also for the errors of his own heart when set alongside – the easy enchantments of lust and loneliness.

Then he took Little Sparrow's hand and together they turned their backs upon that foul forest and everything within it.

As for Baba Yaga and her Sister, perhaps they are still scouring our world, howling out their hatred as they hunt for soft-souled men and their sweet-fleshed daughters. Or perhaps the love-held locks of that comb-cast forest still hold true – I do not know.

THE COAL COMPANION

Jack's time was up. He'd touted and tricked his way across the length, depth and breadth of this world, and all the Other Worlds besides. There was only one road left for him to take and there was no turning back.

It was a cold October evening and dusk was falling as Jack crested the brow of the high hill and the lights of the village unfolded before him, shining bold and bright – like a cache of constellations cradled in the lap of the land.

There at the far side of the valley was his cottage, with smoke pluming from the chimney. Jack could see himself, warming his tired bones by the fire, sharing his mixed fortunes with his Old Mother. He picked up his pace accordingly.

At the bottom of the hill the track curved about a corner and Jack was going too quick to stop himself. There was a big black bag lying in the middle of the path and Jack's boots met it. He went tumbling head over heels and landed up on his back, winded.

Then the bag spoke.

'More haste, less speed, my friend.'

The bag unfolded itself and became a man. He was dressed in a long dark coat and had hair as black as coal.

'There's no getting away from it, Jack,' said the Stranger.

'All your deeds and desires have been weighed up and counted and the scales have fallen accordingly. It's my home, not yours, that we're heading to.'

Jack stood silent for a moment, making his own calculations. Then he grinned.

'Fair's fair,' Jack said. 'Only a fool would try to flee his Fate or fight against it.'

He held out his hand and pulled the Stranger up to full standing.

The Stranger dusted down his coat and fished a tall black hat out of the ditch and fixed it upon his head.

'I have but one favour to ask,' said Jack. 'A drink at the inn before we set out on this great adventure together.'

The Stranger smiled. His teeth were white and sharp.

'Certainly,' he said. 'After all, you have an eternity of hot and thirsty work ahead of you.'

Jack and the Stranger linked arms and they matched stride for stride as they went marching down that dark path into the village. The inn was lit up like a lantern, guiding them in.

When they crossed the threshold, the room fell silent and the faces that turned to them were faces of men that Jack knew. Men he had taunted, thwarted and troubled. Jack had not a single friend amongst them.

The Innkeeper stepped forward, placing one hand upon Jack's elbow and another on the latch of the door.

'It's been quiet times without your company, Jack,' he said. 'And that's the way we're keeping it.'

Jack shrugged aside the hand that held him and slung his arm around the Innkeeper's shoulder.

'It's not trouble I'm bringing,' said Jack. 'But fair reckoning. All the wrongs I've done to all you good folk, I've come to put them right.'

The Stranger slipped away into a dark corner unseen and watched on as Jack emptied his pockets.

There were the lesser grievances and the greater ones, and Jack paid out on all without question.

He paid in coins that were familiar and coins that were not. He paid with the ordinary objects of his trade – the woodknife, the whistle and the whetstone. He paid with the strange articles that he had gathered on his travels – a ruby ring, a golden egg and a fistful of shining black beans. He ordered a flagon of ale for every table, then another and another until all argument was forgotten.

It was a long night and a merry one. But when the first glimmer of dawn came creeping over the hill, the Stranger stepped forward and took Jack's coat from the peg.

Jack turned and whispered into his ear.

'I know, good Sir, that you have a liking for a wager,' said Jack. 'I have a proposition that I think you will find of great interest.'

The Stranger leaned in closer and listened as Jack set out his scheme.

The inn was fit to bursting. Jack had heard tales about the men who had supped at the Stranger's table and the consequences that followed. It was a simple matter of payment of setting the coin that settled the evening's accounts.

The Stranger threw back his head and laughed.

'It takes a Devil to know one,' he said. 'You and I are cut from the same cloth, Jack.'

All that Jack asked of the Devil in return – for the Stranger was indeed none but he – was a little more time in the world that he loved so. A little more adventure and a little more company. Then he would accept the Fate and the fire that was his due.

Jack and the Devil argued out the arithmetic and came to an arrangement. Each man's soul measured out a month. They counted up the crowd and concluded upon ten more years for Jack and a great deal of good sport for the Devil in the meantime.

They shook hands upon the agreement.

Then the Devil turned swiftly on his heel, faster and faster, as if dancing to a wild reel that only he could hear. In the blink of an eye, there was a shifting and shrinking and the Devil was transformed into a golden coin, spinning on the boards at Jack's feet. There caught on the face of it was Satan in his true form: horns, claws, hooves, wings and tail.

Jack held the Devil tight in his fist and made his way over to the Cooper, and in return for another flagon of ale borrowed the use of his hammer and two bracket nails.

In his hand, the Devil kicked and clawed, and the golden coin began to bend and buckle, but Jack held on tight.

Laughing at the absurdity of the instruction, the Cooper hauled Jack up onto his shoulders and carried him through the cheering crowd.

Jack halted him at the threshold. The boundary. The place that was neither in nor out.

His palm began to blister as the golden coin burnt with the heat of the Devil's breath, but still Jack held on tight.

Jack took the coin, the hammer and the nails and set them to the lintel.

Three sharp strikes fixed the first bracket to the horizontal. Three more and the second was set against it crosswise.

'Amen!' cried Jack as he jumped down.

The Devil, caught in the coin within the cage of the crucifix, cursed, cried and pleaded. The drinking men sobered suddenly and were sore afraid.

But Jack stood firm and set the Devil's eternity against his own. He would free the Devil on one condition. That when Jack's time came to depart from this world, the Devil would not claim him. There would be no howling Hell for Jack. He would fashion his own Fate.

The Devil twisted and turned against each and every word, but there was nothing to be done except to swear true to the agreement – before an inn full of wailing witnesses.

Jack prised apart the Devil's fixings. The golden coin fell.

There was a flash of fire and there stood Satan in his full demonic glory, his wings spanning the width of the room and his horns spiking the beams.

He let out a great roar and the boards broke apart beneath the boots of the cowering crowd. The condemned men went hurtling down to Hell, cursing Jack's name as they fell.

The boards snapped shut and there, scattered across the floor of the deserted inn, were all the articles of fortune that Jack had shared out amongst those hundred and twenty simple souls.

Jack filled his pockets and strode out along the empty lanes, laughing all the way to his Old Mother's door.

Jack was not accustomed to living beyond the moment, so whether or not he counted out the passing of the full ten years that followed I do not know.

But one morning, he woke to find the broad blueness of the sky leaching away as he looked upon it, like a lake running dry. The green pastures withered to greyness. The men with whom only the night before Jack had shared food and fire, song and story, turned to ash at his touch.

Then tumbling down into this wide world of nothing came a golden ladder.

Jack set his foot upon the rungs and pulled himself up hand over fist, whistling as he went.

At the top of the ladder there were the gates of pure pearl.

Old Peter was sitting beside them, and they were opened just an inch for a spry Tailor, who slipped through as quick and sharp as a thread through the needle's eye. Jack saw his opportunity, took his hammer from his belt and slung it at the gap to stop it.

Old Peter laughed, and so did the chirruping cherubim at his shoulder.

'It is only through a life of prayer, piety and purpose that a man may enter the Kingdom of God,' he said. 'It is no place for the likes of you.'

Then he took up the hammer and hurled it directly at Jack.

Jack fell head over heels over hammer and landed back in that grey world. That boundary built of mist and melancholy.

It was no dwelling place for a man like Jack. A man made for company and adventure. So he took up his hammer once again and set it to the ash-scaled earth and pummelled away at the land until it broke.

Jack jumped into the cracked chasm and went down laughing.

He landed on a bed of hot coals.

There were the broad black gates. The Devil was sitting beside them, sharpening his instruments.

Jack presented his argument.

The Devil had said it himself, he and Jack were cut from the same cloth and what fine companions they might be, what tricks and tortures might they devise together. Hell was Jack's rightful place and he was ready for it.

The Devil laughed, and so did the ink-eyed imps at his shoulder.

'You would turn my entire empire on its head in an instant, Jack,' he said. 'The nine locks of Hell will remain forever closed against the likes of you.'

The Devil took up a burning coal and hurled it directly at Jack.

The force of the blow threw Jack upwards, back into the pale, dead land.

The chasm sealed shut behind him.

Jack cradled the caught coal to himself for comfort.

Then he saw lying beside him was a dried-up old turnip, the withered stalk sprouting like a tuft of hair from a wrinkled brow.

Jack took out his woodknife and set to work. He carved out his own double, with a great grinning mouth and eyes wide with mirth and mischief.

He set the glowing ember inside the hollow head, tucked it beneath his arm and strode out across the barren land.

Jack still walks that wasteland, pacing out his eternity with his coal companion.

Except for the one night a year where boundaries are broken, thresholds can be crossed and out becomes in.

On All Hallow's Eve, Jack comes creeping, lantern in hand, into the gloomiest places of this world – the depths of the forest, the marshes and the moorlands.

Some folk say that he is offering adventure, lighting the way to buried treasures. Others say that he means to guide us all down to purgatory alongside him for the sake of company.

Only one thing is certain. If you find yourself lost and lonely in the depths of the night and you see a light dancing at the edge of the darkness, best turn your back upon it and walk on.

NOTES ON THE TALES

Lost & Found is my retelling of fifteen treasured folk tales that have nurtured and sustained me, terrified and enthralled me in equal measure.

I grew up in a home steeped in folk tale and folklore. My father, the author Alan Garner, has an extensive research library. My mother, Griselda Garner, is an English teacher and librarian. She actively encouraged me to explore the shelves and find the stories that spoke to me, without any sense of censure of what might or might not be appropriate for a child with a vivid imagination. It is only now, as an adult, that I truly understand what a blessing this was – from both of my parents.

This feeling that the tales are active and alive is something I clearly remember from my childhood. Then, the diverse cast of folk tale characters – the foes and the friends – were my own extraordinary companions as I explored the fields and woods around my local village. The folk tales both enriched the landscape and also enabled me to travel beyond it. I could follow Trickster Jack through his adventures above the world I knew and beneath it; I could ride on the back of the Black Bull of Norroway, across the mountains, as I solved the riddles of the three castles; I could fly above the never-ending pine forests of Russia sitting beside iron-toothed Baba Yaga, the bony-legged witch, riding in her pestle and mortar. I would always get back safely in the end, but I would return home changed.

This personal connection to the tales, rather than any specific cultural origin, source material or story type, is what has dictated the selection. As I wrote, I found that they naturally began to weave themselves together into their own landscape, according to their own laws.

Alongside the folk tales that are taken from those books of my childhood, there are others that I first heard spoken, during evenings spent in the company of many professional storytellers that I have been lucky enough to meet in my adult life, mostly centred around the diverse and dynamic community of The Crick Crack Club. They have always been generous in sharing their source material, true to the oral tradition: the old tales are meant to be passed on to whoever might have use for them.

In the process of research and development, I became fascinated by the echoes of folk tale motifs, oral folklore and the archaeological recorded 'finds' of ritual objects. In this regard, I am hugely indebted to Dr Tim Campbell-Green of The Blackden Trust and The Glossop Cabinet of Curiosities. He has been incredibly generous in sharing his knowledge and research in this specific field.

As such, the title *Lost & Found* reflects a common emotional experience within the collection: the heroes and heroines of the stories who stray from the safer paths in life and find themselves in unknown worlds, which lurk just behind the surface of the world we know. It also reflects the power of the many mysterious objects that are discovered within these adventures, whose purpose is revealed when true magic is most needed. These combine to reveal character: the truth of the inner self that is found when all hope and love seems to be lost.

The more I wrote and the more these lands and tales unfolded with their tests, trials and temptations, the more

I felt that I was back inside the heart of the stories, just as when I was a child, feeling them as direct lived experience. This became the backbone of my retelling: getting under the skin of the characters who could otherwise be thought of as archetypes. What makes Jack the Trickster he is? What is it in the nature of the Youngest Daughter who has the skills to break the complex bonds of the Black Bull's enchantment? What is at the heart of the terrifying power of Baba Yaga, and what human qualities might still yet be able to defeat her?

So it is that whilst folk tales take us beyond our own boundaries into unknown lands, within these adventures, riddles and enchantments we find our common ground. Motifs repeat across stories, subtly varied according to the cultural values and also the landscape of their place of origin, but they are still familiar and speak to our shared humanity.

The 'Three Apples' quote at the start of the collection is an Armenian proverb which I first heard spoken by the wonderful storyteller Vergine Gulbenkian and there is no better way of framing *Lost & Found*. These tales have found their way onto my pages thanks to all the tellers, writers and collectors who stretch back across time. My rewriting is the adding of a voice to a chorus, which grows with each retelling and rereading. We are all links in this chain between past, present and future. Folk tales are tools for living which have survived because they are as relevant now as they ever were, allowing us glimpses of where we might have come from and offering subtle guidance, and occasional warnings, for where we might be going.

THE KING OF THE BIRDS

I cannot recall when I first heard the tale of Wren cheating Great Eagle – it is something that I have known since early childhood. I remember repeatedly trying to seek her out in the woods, following her song but never actually finding her.

When I came to rewrite the story, I went back to Katharine M. Briggs' wonderful *Dictionary of Folk Tales in the English Language* for the source material. The end of the tale is always the same: the concealment, the victory cry of 'Highest it!' and the punishment.

The wren remains a bird that has a reputation for deception. There are theories that in Celtic times it was a sacred bird, and protected – apart from one day a year when a single wren was sacrificed. Later, this became adopted as the Christian tradition of the 'Hunting of the Wren' – the wren reinterpreted as the betrayer of St Stephen, a tradition that still remains today. My ending of the story resets the balance. My wren is the true spiritual helper of mankind, set against the false iconography of the great eagle… and this is an opposition which echoes throughout the collection of tales. The aerial view of the landscape also sets the scene of the 'World Above' landscape of *Lost & Found*.

The calls and language of the rook and the lark were found in fragments, and I wove in the reference to the folk song 'The Lark in the Morning'. I also expanded the opening of the story. In the fragment sources, there is little information about what happens before the declaration of the flying contest, simply the mention of 'after much great debate'. So I went back to Chaucer and revisited *The Parliament of Fowls*. I borrowed the idea of the hierarchy of the birds, the call and response of the debate. I also looked at heraldry, for the variety of the birds used – and then added some creative interpretation of my own. So, the central motif and character reveal of Wren and Great Eagle are true to source... but the build-up to the confrontation is my own flight of fancy, within certain parameters.

THE RIDDLES OF THE CROSSROADS

We move now from the aerial view of the World Above to the direct experience of the earth-bound traveller. Folk tale characters often pass through the crossroads looking for physical and moral direction. As in stories, so in life – crossroads are places loaded with ritual and tradition. Historically, they are where outcasts of society were buried: the executed, the suicides and the witches. The belief was their souls would be confused and unable to find their way to the afterlife. No wonder there is such a strong folklore motif, across story and song, of meeting the Devil at the crossroads. The motif of Jack tricking the Devil also repeats across folk tales. Sometimes he achieves this with physical cunning, sometimes it is linguistic, sometimes a combination of the two. The result is the same: Jack names the Devil and in doing so the Devil reveals his true form; the evil is defeated.

In terms of the source material, the initial riddle of the Henwife is an oral storytelling motif that calls the audience to attention – I first heard it at The Crick Crack Club in London, back in the mid-1990s. 'The Riddles of the Crossroads' song is my own adaptation of the broadside ballad 'A Noble Riddle Wisely Expounded'. The original version is a contest between a Knight (who may or may not be errant) and a Maiden. His questions are seen as a test of her virtue and intelligence. The human qualities and the reveals tend to be the same across variations, although the objects used can differ.

At the heart of this call and response there is transformation: the mundane everyday objects become imbued with power and meaning through the test of looking and retelling. In my work with Dr Tim Campbell-Green, I have been aware of the parallels between this linguistic transformation and the use of everyday objects as protective items in the 'caches' found in old buildings – usually in doorways, chimneys and windows, the boundary places. This is a concept I will refer back to in more detail in my notes on 'Johnnie-He-Not'.

There is no traditional framework for this being Jack's first adventure. However, as mentioned, in all my retellings in the collection I have been drawn to the development of character. Jack is both a familiar folk tale figure and also mercurial. I found myself wondering about the events that formed him – and the crossroads was the obvious starting place. So, the final rewriting and reframing of the riddle into the complexity of Jack's contradictory nature seemed an apposite fit. The end of one story, and the beginning of another...

THE TWISTED OAK

I first encountered this tale in Joseph Jacobs' *English Fairy Tales* as a child: 'Fairy Ointment'. That version is considerably shorter and, in some ways, simpler. An old midwife, Dame Goody, is called upon at night by a 'squinney-eyed, little ugly old fellow' to help his wife. She is taken to a derelict cottage, but when she rubs the ointment in her eye it is transformed into a palace and the ugly boy becomes beautiful. Then she sees the old fellow in the market the following day – he is stealing from the stalls, but this goes unnoticed. She greets him and asks after the child, and he hits her eye and blinds her. There were so many questions for me in this story, not just about the nature of the 'two worlds' but about human nature also. Essentially, why on earth would the midwife risk approaching the old fellow when she was fully aware of who or what he was?

As an adult, tackling the retelling, this question was my way into investigating and expanding the story. Briggs has many versions, and the variation of the reversal of the cottage to palace is fascinating. Sometimes the ointment reveals riches, sometimes it reveals rags. For me personally, the horror of the removal of the eye was so strong that I wanted this to be rooted in the horror of the true vision of the Other World. The replacement of the strike to the eye with the blinding by the bow was a creative leap made due to early collaborations with the fiddle player John Dipper – and it says more about me than it does about him! The location of that world is again rooted in childhood: when I was small, I did have a den in the roots of an oak tree; in my mind it led to a World Below.

Within the oral retellings there is often the sense that this was an experience recounted within the memory of the speaker. In Briggs there was an old woman Joan who suffered this fate. I retold her as a young girl, Jeanie. This was my way of answering that essential question of why she took the risk. The only reasoning that made sense to me was that she must have had a lifetime to forget.

Expanding the timeline of the story gave me the development of the second half of the story: her marriage and her laundering of the false riches. The use of Honesty flowers as the silver coins is again a memory from childhood. My maternal grandmother Betty told me that those seed cases were 'fairy purses' and I saw no reason to doubt it. Perhaps that is indeed where the family fortune came from...

THE WITS OF THE WHETSTONE

I love the challenge of building stories within stories. The collection grew to fit this format: the tales stand alone, but also comment on and echo each other. This tale is the first glimpse of this interweaving world, the gathering of the crowd of characters. It is also the most consciously constructed tale within *Lost & Found*, built on lots of research and forensic attention to structure.

The concept of The Grand Lying Contest is something that I first encountered live at The Crick Crack Club many years ago. There is something truly intoxicating about watching a group of storytellers engaging in the call and response with each other and with the audience as the outrageous energy of the tall tales gathers momentum. The relationship between stories and lies and the role of the Liar as Storyteller is a complex concept that has been debated at length and has many interpretations. However, for me personally it is an exploration of the importance of weighing the values of the 'real world' against the power of the imagination and the belief in the possibilities of the Other Worlds.

In the making of my own contest, I went to Briggs *Part B: Folk Legends* and worked my way through all the recorded narratives of human follies and also the tricksters. As well as the main narratives, every detail of the crowd behaviour is taken from these pages of anecdote or reported tradition. The challenge then was how to pull all these fragments together.

The concept of the Holy Man being declared the best liar in the parish can be found in Briggs and repeats in a few reported tales. Digging a little deeper into background research, I then discovered *The Sermon Upon the Word Malt. Preached in the Stump of a Hollow Tree*. This may sound like the title of a folk tale, but in fact it is printed text by puritan preacher the Rev John Dod (1549–1645). This became the backbone for the story and the language for revealing the preacher as liar. I took the motif of MALT as an acronym, repeated with variation, then threaded it back to the accusations made against the storytelling characters of the Tinker, the Shepherd Boy and Jack.

Jack's alternative beanstalk story was again found in Briggs: a combination of 'The King of the Liars' and 'Jack and the King' – with the role of the listener who is determined not to call out the lie transferred from the King to the Innkeeper. The imagined custom of the inverted pub sign is my own invention – as far as I know! However, once I had established Great Eagle as the figure of external authority in 'The King of the Birds' it only seemed right to turn that world order upside down for the day of misrule.

LITTLE STUPID

This is a story that I first encountered as a child in Arthur Ransome's *Old Peter's Russian Tales*, and I have returned to it repeatedly. Every reading yields more treasures and more questions. It's easy to see common motifs here: the two cruel older sisters, the good-hearted youngest sister who wins the love of the king. However, there is also the over-arching timeframe of seasonal death and rebirth, which brings an additional depth to this tale of the tests and trials of human nature.

In Ransome's collection it is 'The Tale of the Silver Saucer and the Transparent Apple'. For me, in the retelling, it was the interaction between character and object that fascinated. Little Stupid is the name given the heroine of Ransome's story – and her name doesn't change. Not when she is reborn, and neither when she is made Queen. Yet she has clearly shown her intelligence and her integrity by the end of the story.

In some retellings, it's possible to interpret her kindness and her trust in her sisters as her 'stupidity' – but this didn't sit right with me. As any Wise Fool knows, the character who has the ability to transform the everyday object into the magical, whether saucer, apple or a simple reed, may be dismissed by their own society but they are neither foolish nor naïve.

So I went back to Ransome's source: the nineteenth-century Russian collector Aleksandr Afanas'ev. In his retelling the youngest daughter is simply called Fool. However, there is a clear, decisive action that she takes in both versions: the placing of the apple and saucer in her father's care. So, this prompted me to ask the question, 'How did she know to do this?' That question of character and motivation led me to look more deeply into the scrying glass motif of the apple. In both Ransome's and Afanas'ev's versions, it simply shows the wider world beyond the cottage. I took the imaginative leap of it being able to show past, future and present, according to how it was handled. Then everything fell into place. Little Stupid had intelligence, agency and perspective beyond any other character in the story – and this also allowed her to become a powerful queen in her own right.

This scrying development also enabled the wider construction of the book to fall into place. The past and future glimpses that Little Stupid sees in the apple are snapshots of past and future stories at this point in the collection. This was the starting point of the concept of weaving together details of the tales. The appearance of Wren and the Honesty flowers reinvented are my additions, in this context. So, I also learned from Little Stupid: always look at the 'problems' within story and character; therein lies the inspiration and the expansion for the retelling.

LITTLE DOG TURPIE

This was another much-loved tale from childhood, originally titled 'The Hobyahs' from Joseph Jacobs' *More English Fairy Tales*. It was read to me aloud on repeated request – a favourite bedtime story. It also taught me how to read. I can remember chasing the words across the page, alongside JD Batten's wonderful illustrations. His Hobyahs are exactly as described in my retelling when they first emerge from the hempstalks: ink-black imps, tadpole-tailed... They also look like they are having a great time as they riot through the story destroying everything in their path and taking the Little Girl away in the sack. It was the combination of the horror and the gleeful energy that I loved so much – a great combination in any story, but especially in a folk tale.

The original is short and to the point. The chant of the Hobyahs and the dismemberment of Little Dog Turpie carry the narrative drive of the tale and when they get their comeuppance it is swift and effective. In my retelling, I expanded the text by interweaving other folk tale and folklore motifs, whilst still keeping faith with the Hobyahs' story and their world. Again, this came from me actively asking questions of the text and following character logic as I did so.

Firstly, the character of the Little Girl. There are many folk tales where there is an elderly couple with a young child in their care – usually the grandparent/grandchild relationship. So, the absence of definition in Jacobs' tale opened up the possibility of a very different dynamic. Once I researched the means and methods of hemp production, the Little Girl's role fell into place.

Then there was the logic of the Hobyahs manifesting. In the original, they come rampaging out of the hempfield simply because they can. There is a strong folklore motif of the creatures from Other Worlds needing permission to cross the threshold into our world. I invented the Little Girl's responses to the Hobyahs' chant from this premise, using the progressive motif of three: the invitation; the warning; the call for justice. Finally, the fate of Little Dog Turpie in the original is much more brutal: once he has been dispatched by the Old Man he does not come back. Instead, the Tinker has his own dog who gobbles up the Hobyahs. However, the motif of the Magic Bag repeats across folk tales and it has a range of qualities, too many to list here. I gave this particular bag the skill of resurrection, thereby allowing Little Dog Turpie to exact his own revenge – an unexpected hero of the story.

THE ROOTS OF FORTUNE

This is another tale that I first encountered as a child, in Joseph Jacobs' *English Fairy Tales* as 'The Pedlar of Swaffham'. I always loved the folklore magic of the dream voice: the instruction that leads to riches, but not by the obvious route. It never occurred to me that this was a story rooted in real time and real place until I heard oral storyteller Hugh Lupton tell the tale, linking it to the truth of his own known landscape in Norfolk. I was astounded to learn that John Chapman did exist. He was church warden in Swaffham in the 1400s and the church still stands – complete with the carvings in the rooftops and on the pews.

Going back to Briggs, I found further oral tradition verification of the tale. Within this, I also loved the folk tale motifs that were clearly fixed within the narrative – the repetition of the power of three: the three dreams; the three days on London Bridge before the true nature of John's Fate and Fortune is revealed. This became my initial point of expansion for the story. It then felt a natural progression to add references to other characters and objects that travel across the landscape of *Lost & Found* – after all, there's many a long road that leads to London.

In the original tale it is an apple tree that delivers up the riches. However, by the time I came to this retelling I had already written 'The Twisted Oak' and I couldn't resist the echo. In the Briggs sources the Latin inscription on the first pot is mentioned – without the specific words used. The second pot has no instruction, but again following the folklore logic I felt there was space for ambiguity and tension here in the nature of the cost of any otherworldly bargain that leads to riches.

Special thanks must go to Dr Andrew Bell and Dr Richard Ashdowne who provided the Latin translation for my folklore rhymes. Their close attention to phrasing and language use brought yet another dimension to the tale. The translation of the first phrase literally means 'beneath which thing this thing is placed, another rests better than I.' Within this, 'requiescit'/'rests' carries a sepulchral connotation. So, the discovery of the first pot carries a subtle suggestion that disturbing such a thing and indeed profiting from it may be an act of hubris – and there might be consequences. The second phrase is an elegiac couplet, which carries a stern warning indeed: 'Stranger, what profits it all men to have the world's gold when mind and spirit flee your greedy self?'

This in turn led me to the idea of John Chapman's motivation for setting the angels in the rafters having a possible edge of an insurance policy. Then it was a natural development to consider that the pew carvings might be a pious adaptation of the reality of London Bridge – certainly the characters in that crowd would have been both vital and varied.

In Hugh Lupton's retelling, also found in his *Norfolk Folk Tales*, there is a further layer of folklore. The journey becomes a metaphor for human growth and experience: the necessity of the journey away from our roots of birth so that we may return with understanding. The riches that lie in the land we know: our emotional and cultural 'gold in the backyard' are always there – if we have the faith and the courage to dig deep to find them. A philosophy that has certainly proved true to me personally as I have worked on my own process of remembering and retelling these tales.

JOHNNIE-HE-NOT

I have always been fascinated by the motif of the Changeling Child. It repeats across cultures and across time. I do wonder whether it might be a folklore retelling of the common human experience of post-natal depression – or simply the changes of character and behaviour that some babies go through during the early months. I explored this theory within the folk tale backbone of my second novel *The Ingenious Edgar Jones* – but that is, quite literally, another story.

The first written version of the Changeling story I read was 'Brewery of Eggshells' in Joseph Jacobs' *Celtic Fairy Tales* – which varies significantly from this retelling. The Changeling children are twins and the mother is the agent of revelation and eventual return: she uses the trick of the eggshell to discover the true identities. She then throws the 'goblin children' into a lake and her human twins are returned to her. The eggshell is the most common method of discovery I have found in my research. However, alongside the whisky and the bagpipes there are creative uses of pokers and griddle pans and many more besides. There is also a common theme: the Changeling is most regularly disposed of up the chimney.

As previously mentioned in the notes on 'The Riddles of the Crossroads', Dr Tim Campbell-Green and I have discussed the crossover between these variations and the contents of what are thought to be protective 'caches' or 'spiritual middens'. These are everyday objects, which seem to have been deliberately hidden at domestic thresholds: doorways, chimneys, windows. Often these are made of iron: pins, nails, sometimes keys. Alongside them, individual shoes – always worn, always repaired. It's a fascinating echo of story and archaeological object.

Finally, the character who defeats the Changeling is sometimes the Mother, sometimes a Soldier, occasionally a Priest (who makes a sign of the cross from two pokers), but overwhelmingly, it's the Tailor. Perhaps because of the delicate skills required in the brewing of the eggshells. Perhaps because the ability to transform two-dimensional cloth into three-dimensional garments is innately magical.

Tibbie, Johnnie and Wullie are names taken directly from 'The Changeling II', Briggs. Old Wullie's fate is also from Briggs: 'The Tailor and the Fairy' – but this is not an overt Changeling narrative. The Tailor tries to catch a fairy in a bottle but is led away by a beautiful girl in a field who is carrying a blue light. He follows her and is never seen again. It made sense to me that this could be the other side of the Changeling story – the Other Folk can be vengeful, especially against human transgression. So, following the folklore logic I stitched the two tales together into 'Johnnie-He-Not'.

THE BLACK BULL'S BRIDE

If I had to pick a favourite childhood story, this would be the one. Again, I first encountered it in Jacobs' *More English Fairy Tales* as 'The Black Bull of Norroway'. Of course, the Beauty and the Beast motif is clear: the love of the pure-hearted girl transforms the enchanted husband. However, within this, there is so much unusual, fantastic ritual: the red and blue transformations in the grey glen; iron shoes and the glass mountain; the washing of the blood-shirt and the jewels hidden in the fruit.

Again, I began unpacking the details with Dr Tim Campbell-Green. I already understood the significant ritual power of iron from our conversation around Changeling tales. However, historically there were also all sorts of rules around the transformative skills of smelting and metal work: foods that can and can't be eaten; the sequence of making; and most interestingly to me, the exclusion of women from the forge. Tim's own research focused on the cross-cultural concepts of the forge being transformed through ritual into an active, female presence that birthed the iron objects from the 'womb' of the furnace. As such, men were separated from their wives during the smelting process – presumably, there was only space for one powerful woman within the forge at such a spiritually charged and dangerous time.

This gave me a new understanding of the heroine of the story – her tale crosses not only boundaries of real and enchanted landscape, but also the boundaries of culture and ritual. As such, I wanted to give her even more agency and insight. The details of the seven stages of apprenticeship are true to Blacksmith tradition. The song sung in the bedchamber is found in original sources. Her song of the stables was my own invention – threading that motif back.

The original oral source of the story comes from the Scottish

Highlands, according to Briggs. Within this, there are variations – sometimes the fruits are nuts, sometimes eggs. Sometimes the daughters are princesses. Sometimes the King's brothers do not feature. But there is always the glass mountain, the iron shoes, the three visits to the bedchamber to break the enchantment. The Bull, whether Red or Black, always comes from the mysterious land of Norroway.

Then I took a bold leap of imagination. The nearest landmass to the Highlands is the tip of Norway. What if this story travelled along trade routes? What if that glass mountain was a glacier? This led to further expansion of the story. There is indeed a Norwegian custom of the wedding crown, and the values of the jewels revealed in the fruit are true to tradition. I also discovered apposite Norwegian proverbs. *To bite into the sour apple* means to do something you would rather not do. *To be high on the pear* is to have a superior attitude. *To have it as good as the plum in the egg* is to be satisfied. Try as I might, I couldn't fit these into the tale without them seeming imposed. There is no way of proving my 'what if?', of course – but these echoes of proverb and character action within the story are just wonderful and they deserve to be shared.

STEALING THE MOON

The motif of the 'Simpletons' who mistake the reflection of the fallen moon repeats across folklore and can be found in a range of fragment tales in Briggs. There are also continuing traditions across the UK of moonraking festivals – one of the most renowned takes place on alternate years in the Yorkshire village of Slaithwaite in February. It is a week-long event of storytelling and song which culminates in a grand procession down to the canal to retrieve the fallen moon.

In the folklore sources, the moon is sometimes assumed to be cheese, at other times silver. Often it is a simple story of human folly and greed. However, there are examples where Jack is involved in actively tricking the community. This became my starting point for the development of the story.

As mentioned in my notes on 'The Riddles of the Crossroads', I am fascinated by digging a little deeper to explore what makes Jack the character he is. Sometimes the Wise Fool and inevitably the Trickster, Jack always acts out of necessity. His need to follow his own agenda may occasionally cause harm to others, but he is not by nature malicious. So, the first question I asked myself when embarking on this expansion of the motif was what does Jack need, and why?

The five key objects that would give him protection, warmth and wealth became apparent quite quickly. Then I asked myself, who would possess them? Out came the five key characters. Then there came the question, how would Jack persuade such a range of characters to get down that well?

Jack's Trickster behaviour isn't always centred on his own needs. Sometimes he holds a mirror up to human nature – showing other characters their own blindness or hypocrisy. I already knew the Bishop of the Lands from 'The Wits of the Whetstone'. I anchored him and his values at the end of the story and then worked backwards.

Although the association of stock character and specific human folly is my own invention, I also went back to Chaucer again. The tone of the parody here holds echoes of *The Canterbury Tales* – a rich social satire which is also threaded through with folklore motifs. The voice of the storyteller at the end of the piece is the strongest assertion in the collection. It's also the most obvious building of a bridge between the fable and the present day where we find Trickster Jack's lessons are as relevant as they ever were.

THE TROLL KING'S SISTER

Another favourite from childhood – this time taken from *Once Long Ago: Folk & Fairy Tales of the World* retold by Roger Lancelyn Green. This was a book I returned to again and again as a child; it was my first realisation of the relationship between story, landscape and culture. Through this diverse collection I grew to understand that each continent had their own variations of magic and ritual. I also delighted in the rich variety of the Other Folk – both the helpers and those who disrupt the order of our world.

This story comes from Iceland and was originally titled 'The Witch in the Stone Boat'. However, when I revisited the text, it struck me that this was a very specific witch, and this tale of enchantment and deception was a battle between the human World Above and the Troll World Below. Whilst the men may seem to rule the Kingdom, the fight for supremacy and survival is played out between the women. This realisation became my way into the expansion and the retelling of the tale.

In the original version, Sigurd is more observant and assertive – he recognises his True Queen immediately. However, I wanted to explore the idea that this replacement of his wife was a more complex test. As with 'The Black Bull's Bride', if the beloved has been lost and disguised, the journey to reclaim them needs to require character growth and lessons learned. This developed into the investigation of Kingship and Duty.

Also, in the original it is the Prince who constantly draws attention to the deception, in his interactions with the False Queen and with his Nursemaid, so it felt right to give him the ability to tell True from False.

I also changed the stone boat into a millstone, as this echoes motifs found in folklore – the Devil has a millstone that he grinds at the bottom of the sea, but that is a tale to be told in another collection. In addition, I modified the ending. In the original, the Troll King's Sister is placed in a barrel of nails and thrown back into the hole and the danger is over. This didn't quite sit right with me – in folklore the balance between our World Above and the World Below is never fully resolved. It is a constant call and response of guardianship and consequence.

As such, I wanted to hint at an inversion of the Sleeping King motif here, where the hero sleeps beneath the hill until the world is in dire need of him and his army to waken. So, if the hero lies hidden beneath a peaceful land, would not the land above the trapped Witch-Troll be restless?

ASHYPELT

Alongside the Joseph Jacobs' books, I also spent my childhood working my way through the Andrew Lang collections of fairy tales. I first encountered this story in *The Blue Fairy Book* in 'The Tale of a Youth Who Set Out to Learn What Fear Was'. In Briggs, there is a range of fragments and variations on this theme. In some stories Jack is the hero. Ashypelt also appears by name. There is even a version of the charnel house section featuring a heroine: 'The Dauntless Girl'.

In variations of the third trial, the heart of the story is the same: the Wise Fool boy who cannot fear spends three nights in a haunted building. He is visited by various Other Folk and always responds with kindness, cunning and courage – and with a healthy dose of good humour too. This breaks the enchantment of the house and the hero gains riches. Sometimes he also gets a Princess.

In my retelling, a huge part of the enjoyment was stitching together varied details to find my own particular rites of passage for Ashypelt. Specifically, the Phoenix carved on the threshold and the warning it carries only appears in passing in the 'Lousy Jack' tale in Briggs. However, this strong motif of death and rebirth seemed to me to be at the heart of this tale of transformative magic, so it made sense to me that it should manifest again at Ashypelt's moment of victory.

I am fascinated by the idea that to truly grow from boy to man, Fear must be understood. It brings an unexpected element to the concept of the journey of the hero. The motifs of the half-man giant, the skittles game and the coffin-rider repeat across variations. There are also echoes of other stories in *Lost & Found*. Specifically, the chimney as the boundary place chimes directly with the Changeling motif of 'Johnnie-He-Not' – albeit with the 'Other Folk' manifesting on a different scale!

The gaining of the shuddering of Fear is always a coda to the story – the final twist in the tale. In many versions it is a comedy aside: the Princess is so tired of her husband complaining about not knowing how to shudder she throws a cold bucket of water over him when he is asleep. In other versions, she threatens to leave him if he doesn't stop his complaint – and the idea of losing the one he loves brings on the fear. In my retelling, I went back to character, whilst also echoing the tensions of Kingship explored in 'The Troll King's Sister'. Ashypelt – like Jack, in his versions of the story – is defined by his free spirit, his mischief and his rule-breaking.

It seemed to me that for such a young man, the burden of Kingship would be the most terrifying Fate of all...

JUST JIMMY

This tale is unique within the collection in that I have only ever heard it told. It features in the brilliant collaborative show *The Sleeping King*, by Hugh Lupton, Daniel Morden and Nick Hennessey. This is an interweaving of tales centred on the motifs of the sleeping hero and the hidden worlds that sit side by side with the world we know. Within this, Daniel Morden tells the tale of 'The Man With No Story to Tell'. Daniel informs me that he first heard the story from the traveller and storyteller Betsy Whyte – best known for her autobiography *The Yellow on the Broom*, published in 1979. I couldn't trace the ultimate origin of the story, but as it comes from Betsy's canon I can only assume that it is very old indeed.

In my research, I found the motif of gender transformation in tales of other cultures – in Hindu mythology especially. In this context, the transformation often happens in or around a body of water. I haven't been able to find any British counterparts or variations of this particular tale – but that may well be due to the limitations of my own research, rather than an empirical fact.

In 'The Man With No Story to Tell', protagonist Jimmy is looking for shelter and he finds himself in a house where food and lodging is exchanged for a story. When he declares he has no story to tell, the host gives him a thimble and instructs Jimmy to use it to empty the nearby lake... and so his adventure begins. By the time I started working on my retelling, The Grand Lying Contest had already been anchored in the collection in 'The Wits of the Whetstone' – so it felt right that Jimmy should stumble into that tale, enabling us to consider that fascinating relationship between Storyteller and Liar from a completely different angle.

The replacement of the story with the lie then cemented Jimmy's character for me – and allowed me to play with his dialogue too. I also loved playing with the Cinderella motif ever so slightly, bringing a new context to that well-known story! In the conclusion of 'The Man With No Story To Tell', Jimmy's Youngest Daughter goes missing and Jimmy gets lost in the search for her, and this creates the return to the lake. The addition of the White Stag is my own invention. However, it is also a strong folklore motif that repeats across cultures. The White Stag is a sacred creature. It is a symbol of change and the quest to hunt it is a quest of spiritual discovery. Within this, there is the lovely paradox that whoever slays the White Stag will be cursed with bad luck. These concepts seemed to me to be at the heart of this tale of transformation, and as such an appropriate catalyst for both the start and the end of Jimmy's adventures in the Other World.

LITTLE SPARROW

I can't remember not knowing about Baba Yaga, the bony-legged iron-toothed witch who lives in a house on chicken legs and who rides out in a pestle and mortar. My maternal grandfather Paul had Russian roots, but he died when I was young. Perhaps he told me about Baba Yaga. Perhaps she is a character that was passed down to my mother and that's how I heard about her. I first read about her in Ransome's *Old Peter's Russian Tales*, where this tale was named 'Baba Yaga and the Little Girl with the Kind Heart'.

As with my retelling of 'Little Stupid', I was interested in giving the female protagonist more complex character traits, whilst still keeping true to the narrative of the original. In Ransome's text the stories are framed by the grandfather Peter telling the tales to his grandchildren – whom he refers to as his 'Little Pigeons'. This led me to think about renaming and personalising the little girl. Just as with 'The King of the Birds' I went back to the symbolic qualities of birds. The sparrow is small but powerful. A symbol of joy, creativity and protection. There is also the association of a dual nature: hard-working, but takes life lightly. The character of my Girl with the Kind Heart was thus anchored and named – and these qualities then became threaded through my expansion.

I also researched Russian proverbs. *The morning is wiser than the evening* and *Not all questions bring good* are true to the culture. The latter also extends with the line *Get and know much and old soon you'll grow* – which I then rewrote into the apple/tree rhyme. The further anchoring of the story around the concept of the two sides to any situation, or indeed character, was my own focus – and it's an idea that echoes through *Lost & Found*. It's also there in the wider context of the Baba Yaga tales, of which there are many. She may be a child-eating Witch, but she can also use her powers to help heroes and heroines whom she deems worthy. But those are stories for another collection.

The 'two sides' is also there in the power of the magical objects of comb and shawl, which always delighted me as a child. I took some creative licence in the creation of the third magical object of the needle and thread – thus completing the pattern of three inherent in folk tale structure. I also drew on wider folklore association of the witch. Their limbs can grow back. They can be revealed by looking through a hag stone. Combining these elements into the return home with the bone needle and hair thread was my final element of pulling together this retelling, giving Little Sparrow courage and cunning, alongside her kindness, as a means of revealing the truth of her experience.

THE COAL COMPANION

Having anchored Jack's first adventure at the start of *Lost & Found* the collection was always going to end with the revelation of Jack's final Fate. The heart of this story is the old Irish tale 'Stingy Jack'. It travelled to the USA with the first wave of immigration and the turnip transformed into the pumpkin accordingly. I also find it fascinating how the meaning of the lantern has shifted. The lantern has become Jack, and it is seen as a symbol of evil. However, it could also be argued that the placing of the carved heads in the windows could be a protective act. As detailed in the notes on 'Johnnie-He-Not', the window is another boundary place, a weak point in the house. The jack-o'-lantern could be seen to be warding off evil, scaring away the Devil – as with gargoyles on churches.

There are variations of 'Stingy Jack' that can be found in various retellings and are closely documented in Briggs. The backbone of the story is the same: Jack tricks the Devil, bargains for ten more years and then finds himself stuck in-between Heaven and Hell. In some versions Jack does indeed help the Devil gather more souls over time – I simply made him more efficient by allowing that to play out in the inn.

I find the detail that the Devil becomes a coin absolutely fascinating. Again, in conversation with Dr Tim Campbell-Green, we have discussed his archaeological finds of bent coins: currency thus transformed into votive objects, protective items or indeed love tokens. Perhaps the Devil in the coin is a folk tale inversion of that ritual. Sometimes Jack carves a cross on the coin; sometimes he places the coin next to a cross in his pocket. It was my invention to place it in the crucifix of nails at the boundary place – again echoing that idea of iron as both protective and transformative.

This also links nicely to 'The Smith and the Devil' variation in Briggs, where I found the details of Jack throwing the hammer at the gates of Heaven – in the moment where the Tailor slips in. I would like to think that could be Old Wullie, having escaped whatever punishment was meted out to him by the Changeling folk... but I will leave that for the readers to decide.

BIBLIOGRAPHY

FOLK TALES: PRIMARY SOURCES

Afanas'ev, Aleksandr
Russian Fairy Tales
Translated by: Guterman, Norbert
Pantheon (1976)

Briggs, Katharine M.
Dictionary of Folk Tales in the English Language
Part A: Folk Narratives
Part B: Folk Legends
London: Routledge and Kegan Paul (1970–1971)

Jacobs, Joseph
English Fairy Tales
David Nutt (1890)

Jacobs, Joseph
Celtic Fairy Tales
David Nutt (1892)

Jacobs, Joseph
More English Fairy Tales
David Nutt (1894)

Lancelyn Green, Roger
Once Long Ago: Folk and Fairy Tales of the World
Golden Pleasure Books (1962)

Lang, Andrew
The Blue Fairy Book
Longmans, Green & Co (1889)

Lupton, Hugh
Norfolk Folk Tales
The History Press (2013)

Ransome, Arthur
Old Peter's Russian Tales
Nelson (1916); Puffin Books (1974)

COMPANION TEXTS

Chaucer, Geoffrey
The Canterbury Tales
Translated by Nevil Coghill
Penguin Classics (2003)

Chaucer, Geoffrey
The Parliament of Fowls
Translated by Simon Webb
Langley Press (2016)

Dod, Rev John
A Sermon Upon the Word Malt. Preached in the Stump of a Hollow Tree
Gale Ecco (2018)

RESEARCH & REFERENCE

Travers, P.L.
What The Bee Knows: Reflections on Myth, Symbol and Story
Penguin Books (1993)

Brewer, Ebenezer Cobham
Revised by Evans, Ivor H.
Dictionary of Phrase and Fable
Cassell & Co (1970)

Wilson, Stephen
The Magical Universe: Everyday Ritual and Magic in Pre-Modern Europe
Hambledon and London (2000)

Zipes, Jack
The Great Fairy Tale Tradition
W. W. Norton & Company (2001)

WEBSITE REFERENCES

The Blackden Trust
www.theblackdentrust.org.uk

Crick Crack Club
www.crickcrackclub.com

Dr Tim Campbell-Green
The Glossop Cabinet of Curiosities
www.glossopcuriosities.wordpress.com

ACKNOWLEDGEMENTS

These tales do not belong to me. They have travelled many long roads before they made it to my door, across the threshold and onto the page. I have a deep debt of gratitude to all those, unnamed and unknown, who told the tales before me.

I also am indebted to my parents, Alan and Griselda Garner, who allowed me free rein of their bookshelves and libraries from a young age. Nothing was forbidden, and everything was discussed. I am equally grateful to my uncle, Gilbert Greaves, whose generous support over the years has enabled me to build my own library of folk tales and research – without which *Lost & Found* would not be the book it is.

No lesser debt is to the storytellers that I have been lucky enough to encounter in childhood, and whose tales have sustained me ever since. My inner life would have been so much poorer without this community. Specific thanks to Ben Haggarty who, twenty years ago now, gave me space, time and support when I first began setting pen to page. The members of The Crick Crack Club who gathered along the way and shared their stories and good company: Vergine Gulbenkian; Emily Hennessey; Nick Hennessey; Daniel Morden. Special thanks also to Hugh Lupton for the thoughtful and inspiring foreword.

Thank you to Phoebe Connolly, whose call and response illustrations have brought depth and dimension to the world of the tales. Her craft and attention to detail have been astounding to witness.

Thank you to John Dipper and Dave Malkin, who encouraged me to write, develop and perform these tales alongside them. Their creative company on the stage is always a delight and has enabled me to find a voice and confidence that would have been impossible otherwise.

Thank you to Finn and Lilah Heywood-Sethi, who listened to the tales in progress and asked all the difficult questions that I needed to hear. The world of the book is richer and wilder due to their deep, intuitive and playful understanding of story and myth.

Thank you to all at Unbound for the faith in the book and all the hard work in bringing it into being. Lizzie Kaye for the initial launching of the project. John Mitchinson for the support in every aspect of the book's evolution. Rachael Kerr for the eagle-eyed development edits on the text. Georgia Odd and Becca Harper-Day for steering me through the process of online crowdfunding. DeAndra Lupu for editorial management and patience. Mark Ecob for cover design. Hayley Shepherd for the meticulous copy edit.

To all the subscribers, my most sincere thanks. This book would simply not exist without you.

Thanks also to Jessica Woollard for managing all the practicalities whilst I was weaving the tales together.

The world of *Lost & Found* may seem other and unknown, but it sits upon a bedrock of historical research and close attention to the puzzles of the past. For this, my deepest thanks to Dr Tim Campbell-Green, Dr Andrew Bell and Dr Richard Ashdowne. Any errors or implausible leaps of the imagination are entirely my own.

Last but by no means least, I would not have made it through the tangled woods of *Lost & Found* and home again without my Extraordinary Companion, Al Kenny. Thanks for all the support, the laughter and the adventures.

A Note on the Author

Elizabeth Garner is the author of two novels, *Nightdancing* and *The Ingenious Edgar Jones*, both of which were influenced by traditional folk tale narratives and motifs. *Lost & Found* is her first collection of rewritten stories.

She studied English literature at Oxford University and worked as a film script editor for a variety of European and US production companies. She now works as a freelance fiction editor, teaches creative writing and is the arts trustee at the Blackden Trust, an educational charity established at her family home in Cheshire.

www.elizabethgarnerauthor.co.uk

A Note on the Illustrator

Phoebe Connolly was born in Sussex in 1997, where she grew up in a house full of animals, art and books, surrounded by the South Downs and coast. She studied at West Dean College of Arts and Conservation, graduating in 2020. Working across a number of mediums, she has developed a passion for engraving, working with line and light to capture fleeting imagery on surfaces as diverse as paper, wood, metal and glass. Her illustrations for *Lost & Found* were engraved on endgrain blocks and handprinted on an 1840s book binders Imperial press.

Unbound is the world's first crowdfunding publisher, established in 2011.

We believe that wonderful things can happen when you clear a path for people who share a passion. That's why we've built a platform that brings together readers and authors to crowdfund books they believe in – and give fresh ideas that don't fit the traditional mould the chance they deserve.

This book is in your hands because readers made it possible. Everyone who pledged their support is listed below. Join them by visiting unbound.com and supporting a book today.

Geoff Adams
Karen Aicher
Hilary Alcock
Hazel Alexander
Ali Ali
Ashley Allen
Vicky Allen
David Almond
Kerry Aluf
Family Anderson
Neil Anderson
Angie Arnold
Arthur, Wilf & Peggy
Wendy Ashley
Carl Ashworth
Afroze Asif
Gordon Askew

Rosemary Athayde
James Attlee
James Aylett
Yaba Badoe
Duncan Bailey
Julie Bailey
Tim Bailey
Duncan Baines
Ami Baker
Martin Baker
Katy Balagopal
Miranda Ballesteros
Jason Ballinger
Dr. Roger Barberis
Sara Barratt
Rick Bateson
Emma Bayliss

Val Bayliss-Brideaux

Vikki Bayman

Simon Baynes

Bob Beaupre

Lil Bee

Andrew Bell

Seona Bell

Ronnie Bendall

Paul Victor Bennett

Julia Benning

Sarah Benton

Stephanie Benvenuto

Ari Berk

Adam Bertolett

Steve Besley

Miranda Bird

Heather Blanchard

Heather Anne Blankenship

Graham Blenkin

Pat Bomford

James Boocock

Charles Boot

Anne Booth

Alexander Borg

Wendy Bosberry-Scott

Chris Bostock

Mary Bownes

Angela Boyden

Matt Bradbury

Hannah Brailsford

David Bramwell

Alan Brannon

Claire Braven

Richard W H Bray

Lisa Brice

J Briggs

Lindsey Brodie

Claire Broughton

Camilla Brown

Emma Brown

Nicky Brown

Andrea Burden

Geoff Burton

Rosemary Burton

Gillian Butler

Ariell Cacciola

Regina Caldart

Nick Campbell

Tim Campbell-Green

Xander Cansell

Ian Capes

Leah Carden

Jonquil Cargill

Bill Carmichael

Jane Carter

Nicholas Carter

Rose Cartwright

Sally Chandler

John Luke Chapman

Andy Charman

Jane Churchill

Indigo Clardmond

Lucy Claridge

Daniella Clark

Amanda Clarke
Fiona Clarke
Valerie Clarke
Vanessa Clarke
Mathew Clayton
Simon Clements
Gill Clifford
Garrett Coakley
Persephone Coelho
Daniel Cohen
Gina Collia
Fiona Colliins
Sarah Easter Collins
Mary Compton-Rickett
Dom Conlon
Amanda Connolly
Penny Coombes
Helen Cooper
Andrew Correia
Geoff Cox
Robert Cox
Tina & Mike Crawley
Marise Cremona
Sarah Crofts
Andrew Croker
CrystalLakeManagment
Pamela Cullen
Kristofer Cullum-Fernandez
Daniel Cyphus
Profs Bob Cywinski & Sue
    Kilcoyne
Kelly A. D'Ambrosio

Dylan D'Arch
Raluca David
Alexander Davidge
Stuart Davidson
Victor Davidson
Steph Davies
Joshua Davis
Laura Davis
Andrew Davison
Sarah Day
Bastiaan De Zwitser
Dedicated to West
    Dean College
Jane Dee
Karen Delaney Gifford
Philippe Demeur
J Dennison
Ted Dewan
Silvia Di Blasio
Sara "Willie" Didier
Glenn Dietz
Louise Diggins
John Dipper
Cathy Dixon
Emma Dobell
Richard Dobell
Therese Doherty
Natalia Dominguez
Maura Dooley
Emma Dougherty
Linda Doughty
Jacqueline Drake

Jen Drake
Rebekah Drury
Helena Duk
Daniel Early
Elizabeth East
Jenny Echevarria - Lang
Mark Edmonds
Birgit Einhoff
Melissa Elischer
Patricia Elliott
David Ellis
Maggie Ellis
E England
Darren Ettle
Patricia Evans
Karen Faiers
Vogel Family
Georgia Fancett
Finbarr Farragher
Louise Farrow
Anna Farthing
Tony Felgate
Clair Fellows
David Felton
Natalie Fernandes
Wes Finch
Val Finnegan
Colin Fisher
James Flannery
Sam Fleming
Maximilien Fleuriot-Reade
Jane Flynn

Stuart Forbes
Carolyn Fordham
Penelope Foreman
Chris Fosten
Jodie Francis
Philippa Francis
Julian Francis-Lawton
Sarah Fraser
Siobhan Fraser
Kerena Fussell
Matthew Gabrielli
Caroline Gale
Antonia Galloway
Alan & Griselda Garner
Joe Garner
Joseph Garner
Sam Garner
Tom Garner
Alasdair Garnham
John Garth
Lynn Genevieve
Valerie Gianoli
Matthew Gibbons
Hannah Gibson
Lyn Gibson
Julie Giles
Catriona Gilkes
Jonathan Gill
Steve Gladwin
Catherine Glenday
David & Marion Goda
Susan Godfrey

Stephanie Goldberg
Tim Goodall
Victoria Goodbody
Jess Gordon
Venetia Gosling
Juliette Gray
Gilbert Greaves
Jennifer Green
Malcolm Green
Mary-Rose Grieve
Gail Griffin
Jane Griffin
Cathy Griffiths
Mike Griffiths
Clare Grist Taylor
Vergine Gulbenkian
Philippa Gurney
Laura Gustine
Ben Haggarty
Carole Hailey
Jenny Hall
Verity Halliday
Matthew Hancock
Jeremy Hanks
Jess Hannar
Alison Hardy
Hilary Harley
Andrea Harman
Jac Harmon
Tim Harper
Paul Harris
Lynne Harrower

Graham Harvey
James Harvey
Elspeth Head
Jane Healy
Andrew Hearse
Meryl Heath
Oliver Heath Hinds
Margot Heesakker
Andrea Heffernan
David and Alison Heke
Nick Hennessey
Lee Henshaw
Lucy Henzell-Thomas
Lu Hersey
Cecilia Hewett
Gail Hewitt
Liz Heywood
Amanda Hickey
Jonathan Hill
Gabriel Henry Hinds
Julie St Claire Hoare
Barbara Hockley
Holly Hodson
Andrea Holland
Samantha Holland
Caroline Hollick
Michael Holliman
Wayne Hollis
Fran Holmes
John R Holmes
Fiona Hope
Michael Horsley

Eric Horstman
Katy Hoskyn
Lucy Hounsom
Antony Howard
Jo Howard
Sara Howard
Alan Howe
Joe Howsin
JoAnne Hughes
Nicola Hughes
Tom Hughes
Ken Hunt
Jessica Hurtgen
Samantha Hutton
Carole Hyman
Ben Illis
Scott Innes
Brent Isaacs
Joel Iseli
Farah Ismail
Diana Jackson
Kathy Jackson
Michelle Jana Chan
Ben Jeapes
Christian Jeffery
Simon Jerrome
Noelia Jiménez Martínez
Heather Jobling
Andy Johnson
Alice Jolly
Brian Jones
Kathy Jones

Laura Jones
Raymond Jones
Siân Jones
Mary Jordan-Smith
Franziska Jörg
Peter Jukes
Sarah Kafala
Sophie Kaiser
Amit Kamal
Milan Karol
Sonia Kaur
KC KC
Peter Kelly
Nidge Kendrick
Helen Kennedy
Al Kenny
Rachael Kerr
Carol Kerry
Mary Kersey
Dan Kieran
Isobel Kieran
Ruth Killick
Steve Killick
Eleanor King
Robert Kinns
Jessie Kitchens
Daniel Kleinman
Jennie Knight
Stephanie Kovacs
Carina Krause
Helene Kreysa
Kristine Loeb Krozek

Philip Henry Krozek
Terry Kuny
Mit Lahiri
Gill Laker
Anne Lane
John S. Langley
Katherine Langrish
Nick Lansbury
Sue Lansbury
Anna Lawrence
Jennifer Lawson
Freya Marie Lawton
Alison Layland
Simone Layton
Colin Le Good
Caroline Lee
Ruth Leonard
Julie Lerwill
Alick Leslie
Alison Levey
Simon Lewis
Jonathan Light
Aldona Likus
Johanna Lilley
Sylvia Linstead
Rosa Little
Amy Lloyd
Andrew Lockhart
Eleanor Violet Locock-Jones
Johanna Lohrengel
Lady Lothian
Stephen Lunn

Hugh Lupton
Mike Lynd
Seonaid Mackenzie
Seonaid Mackenzie-Murray
Steven Maddocks
Gregory Maguire
Sharon Maguire
Phil Mahoney
Kizzy Makinde-Corrick
Daniel Malin
Dave Malkin
Philippa Manasseh
Neal Mann
Rachael Mannie
Zed Marsh
Anna Martin
Bee Martin
Kerry Martin
Mandy Martinez
Lu Mason
Lydia Massiah
Mark Masterson
David Matkins
John Matthews
Camilla May
Sean McCann
Yvonne Carol McCombie
Matilda McDermott
Martine McDonagh
Hazel McDowell
Fiona McGavin
Karen Rosemary Mckee

Kerry McKenna

Amanda McLachlan

Brian Mcleish

Christine Mcmahon

Arran Meachim

Alice Meadows

Susan Meikle

Ian Mella

Susan Memmott

Eleanor Mercer

Anne Merwynne

Kristina Meschi

Diana Metcalfe

Jenny Metson

Kizzia Mildmay

Caroline Miles

Kirsty Miles

Claire Miller

Andrew Millington

John Mitchinson

Banibandana Mohapatra

Richard Montagu

Penny Montague

Ange Mooney

Paula Moorhouse

Amanda Moron-Garcia

Jackie Morris

Jane Morris

Morgan Morris

Mary Moss

Bernard Moxham

Rebecca Moyle

Dwina Murphy-Gibb

Barbara Murray

Stu Nathan

Carlo Navato

Christopher Nelson

Briony Newbold

Rosalind Newcomb

Alison Newman

Haulwen Nicholas

Sue Nichols

Aer Nicholson Clasby

Bodenham Nicola

Pascale Nicolet

Alexander Nirenberg

Sally Norris

Lesley Northfield

Louise Northway Norman

Sakthi Norton

Conrad Nowikow

Andrew Nunn

Nina O'Connor

Ruth O'Leary

Ros O'Sullivan

Helen Oakman

Kevin Offer

Claire Ogden

Kathy Oh

Eva Ontiveros

Angela Osborne

Vita Osborne

Jamie Owen-John

Scott Pack

Julia Parker

Katharine Parker

Edward Parnell

Dawn Parry

William James Parry

Kate Parsons

James Patterson

Natalia Peace

Lisa Pearce Collins

Esme Pears

Paul Pearson

Joe Peepos

Jayme Pendergraft

Chris Pennell

Oonagh Pennington-Wilson

Amanda Percy

Anna Perdibon

Helen Perry

Lisa Petronzio

Katie Phelps

Neil Philip

Liz Phillips

Mark Phillips

Chantelle Pike

Alison Pinder

Andrew Plant

Justin Pollard

Dorota Pomorska-Dawid

Ann-Marie Pond

Holly Potier

Richard Potts

Emma Pounds

Robert & Babs Powell

Victoria Powell

Nita Prakash

Richard Prangle

Janet Pretty

Barney Price

Tina Price-Johnson

Thea Prothero

Donald Proud

Claire Pulford

Jude Pullman

Caroline Pulver

Christiane Purcell-Wells

Lisa Quigley

Danielle Quinn

Christopher Rasmussen

Anastasia Ratcliffe

Chris Ratcliffe

Sophie Ratcliffe

Colette Reap

Jenny Reddish

El Redman

Andrea Reece

Harriet Reed

Ian Rees

Chris Richards

Emily Richards

Alexandra Richiteanu

Liam Riley

Geri Rinna

Nicole Rivette

Ian Robb

Karen Roberts

Mark Roberts

Gareth Robinson

Lola Robinson

Richard Robinson

Tom Roper

Kalina Rose

Tamsin Rosewell

Andy Rouillard

Alexandra Rowlands

Charlie Rowlands

Gill Ryan

SF Said

Ellen Sandberg

Peter Sanham

Mike Sansbury

Jemma Saunders

Danny Scheinmann

Gabriel Schenk

Julia Schlotel

Lisa Schneidau

Janette Schubert

Candy Schwartz

Jenny Schwarz

George Peter Martyr Scott

Matthew Scott

Rosemary Scott

Nina Seale

Kabir Sethi

Belynda J. Shadoan

Eric Shaffstall

Harriet Shannon

Deborah Siddoway

silhouby

Damian Silverton

Chris Simmonds

Dan Simpson

Joe Skade

Catherine Smillie

Alan Smith

Helen Elizabeth Smith

Kirsty Smith

Lorraine Smith

Lyndsey Smith

Michael Smith

Nick Smith

Valarie Smith

Michael Smith &
        Nicky Parker

Ali and Sarah Smith and Wood

Marilyn Sneddon

Jayne Southern

R Spackman

Ben Spencer

Teresa Squires

Charlotte Stark

Sean Steele

Gabriela Steinke

David Stevens

Carol Stone

Corinne Stone

Pernille Strande

Ellen Stratton

Torkjell Stromme

Christopher Stuart
Julie Stuart
Nina Stutler
Robert Swann
Gareth Sylvester-Bradley
Mark Symons
Anne Tame
John Tarrow
Elspeth Tavaci
Abby Taylor
Georgette Taylor
Benjamin Tehan
The Library, University
    College Oxford
Karen Theilade
Caroline and Buddhashanti
    Thickbroom
Emma Thimbleby
Adam Thomas
Ian Thomas-Bignami
A.R. Thompson
Dominic Thompson
Helen Thompson
Laura Thompson
Liz Thompson
Rebekah Thompson
Catherine Thorn
Christopher Thornton
Adam Tinworth
Kathryn Tipping
Mat Tobin
Sef Townsend

Lindsay Trevarthen
Melina Trixas
Jacqui Trowsdale
Christie Tucker
Jo Tucker
Ann Tudor
Tim Turan
Tim & Ro Turan
Ron & Judy Turbin
Karen Turner
Anne Marie van Es
Davy Van Obbergen
Charles Vane
Maria Vatanen
Stephanie Vendryes
Elizabeth Verbraak
Ashley Vine
Stephanie Volk
Ruth Vorstman
Erica Wagner
Judy Walker
Sir Harold Walker
Stephen Walker
Tony Walker
Peter Walker-Birch
Susan Walmsley
Nick Walpole
Eleanor Walsh
Chee Lup Wan
Miranda Ward
Annabel Wardrop
Lora Waring

Olivia Watchman
Anne Watson
Nathan Weber
Deborah Weir
Julie Weir
Alexandra Welsby
Jordan Welsh
Helen Wendholt
Celine West
Elizabeth West
Penelope West
Katie Weston
Jane Wheeler
Georgina White
Jo White
Susan White
Miranda Whiting
Freya Widdicombe
Nick Wilcox

Suzie Wilde
John Wilkinson
Dawn Will
Emma Williams
Catherine Williamson
Catherine Williamson
Dawn Wilson
Derek Wilson
Ed Wilson
Howard Wix
Valerie Wolf
Estelle Wolfers
Philip Womack
Lucy Wood
Peter Wood
David Wooldridge
Isabelle Woollard
Erin Wyatt